SHAKESPEARE PUZZLES

CEDRIC WATTS

PublishNation

Copyright © Cedric Watts, 2014.

ISBN: 978-1-291-66410-2

PublishNation, London.

Contents:

1. Introduction. — 5
2. Shakespeare's Sonnets: Not Autobiographical? — 8
3. *The Taming of the Shrew*: Why is It Allowed? — 13
4. What is the Plot of *Love's Labour's Won*? — 17
5. *Love's Labour's Lost*: An Illogical Title? — 21
6. Why do Romeo and the Friar Utter the Same Speech? — 26
7. Why does Juliet say 'Romeo' when she means 'Mountague'? — 31
8. Does Shakespeare Condemn Extra-Marital Copulation? — 36
9. A Bum Rap? In *A Midsummer Night's Dream*, Does 'Bottom' Mean 'Bum'? Bottom's Name Anal-ysed. — 40
10. Who is the 'Manager of Mirth'? In *A Midsummer Night's Dream*, Act 5, is It Philostrate or Egeus? — 47
11. Vanishing Trick in *A Midsummer Night's Dream*: Where is the Wedding Song? And Why is Recycling Apt? — 51
12. The Mysterious Mobility of Salarino. — 55
13. The Puzzle of the Two Hals in *Henry IV, Part 2*. — 59
14. Should We Save Innogen in *Much Ado about Nothing*? — 64

15. Banish the Sentimentalists' Claudio! The Puzzle of *Much Ado about Nothing*, Act 5, scene 3.	68
16. 'Dauphin' or 'Dolphin' in *Henry V*?	72
17. Brutus: Hypocritical Stoic?	76
18. *Hamlet* or *Hamleth*?	81
19. Malvolio's Revenge: What is It?	86
20. The Puzzle of the 'Willow Song' in *Othello*.	90
21. *Othello*: Can Impossibility Increase Empathy?	94
22. What are the 'Glass Eyes' in *King Lear*?	99
23. Who is the 'Poor Fool' in *King Lear*, Act 5?	104
24. 'Faith, here's an equivocator': in *Macbeth*, is It Shakespeare?	108
25. Is Axing 'a Wife' a Feminist Act? A Notorious Puzzle in *The Tempest*.	112
26. Prospero's Epilogue: is It Really Shakespeare's Farewell?	118
Acknowledgement.	126

1

Introduction.

This book tackles a range of puzzles presented by Shakespeare's works. These puzzles provide some informative entertainment. We find repeatedly that apparently small matters have big implications. What looks like a matter of detail often opens up a large area of possibilities.

For instance, the matter of the 'glass eyes' in *King Lear* expresses the play's great theme of injustice and hypocrisy in high places (always a topical matter). Another example is this: as soon as you think about the strangely variable era depicted in *Hamlet* – is the action set in ancient times or recent times? – the whole play seems to split and transform itself, as does its hero. Then there's Shakespeare's long-lost comedy, *Love's Labour's Won*: what was in it? (With a bit of ingenuity, we can specify the contents in considerable detail.)

The other items take us on an exploration – in more or less chronological order – of numerous plays and poems by the Bard, bringing to light, for instance, the Dolphin of *Henry V,* suppressed Innogen (the missing mother) of *Much Ado*, and Shakespeare himself (disguised as Prospero) in the Epilogue of *The Tempest*.

Of course, the book maintains the traditional but often challenged belief that the works usually attributed to Shakespeare were predominantly by Shakespeare. The first puzzle, on the sonnets, gives various reasons for this. Orthodox scholars agree that some of the works (*Titus Andronicus* and *Macbeth*, for instance) contain small amounts of material by other writers. A couple of the odder plays, *Pericles* and *Timon*, were certainly collaboration-jobs, and in those two works the collaborators have been identified as George Wilkins and Thomas Middleton respectively. John Fletcher contributed largely to *Two Noble Kinsmen* and *Henry VIII*, and Shakespeare was one of several writers of *Henry VI, Part 1*.[1]

Nevertheless, the notion that Shakespeare was merely an uncouth front-man, a talentless conduit, for works produced by some mysterious genius, can amply be refuted. Postulated rival contenders for the authorship include: the Earl of Oxford (advocated in the 2011 film *Anonymous*), Christopher Marlowe, Lord Bacon, Queen Elizabeth, and even a committee of numerous writers. There's something suspicious about the list. All these contenders were either aristocrats, or university-educated, or both. The implication is that a glover's son from Stratford upon Avon, who never went to university, just wasn't capable of writing the greatest body of plays the world has known. Basically, the case for a rival author rests mainly on snobbery.[2]

In fact, Shakespeare worked for many years as actor, script-writer and shareholder with a leading company; so, if he had been an impostor, his fellow-actors would soon have found out. There is plenty of documentary evidence confirming that Shakespeare's theatrical career was remarkably successful; and the First Folio, the first collected edition of the works, is a handsome tribute to the Bard from his erstwhile colleagues. Furthermore, as Chapter 2 shows, those sonnets give poignant reminders of the personal vicissitudes of the man who repeatedly puns on the name 'Will'.

The plays and poems offer an abundance of mysteries and riddles. That's one of the facts which keep the Shakespeare industry alive and thriving. And it's one of the reasons why people repeatedly see the plays and read the poems. With Shakespeare, there's always something new to be done, some new discovery to be made. It's largely his combination of eloquent authority and peculiar puzzles that keeps his works alive. And some solutions to those 'peculiar puzzles' ensue.

Notes:
1. See Brian Vickers: *Shakespeare, Co-Author: A Historical Study of Five Collaborative Plays* (Oxford: Oxford University Press, 2002).

2. See James Shapiro: *Contested Will: Who Wrote Shakespeare?* (London: Faber and Faber, 2010).

2

Shakespeare's *Sonnets*: *Not* Autobiographical?

The eminent Shakespeare scholar, Professor Jonathan Bate, says that when he re-reads the *Sonnets*, he always tells his students and himself that 'the opposition between dark lady and fair youth' should be regarded as 'a dramatic device': 'one is a "character" representing desire in its sexual manifestation, the other in its idealizing and spiritual'. His general advice about the sequence of sonnets is: 'Don't be drawn into the trap of supposing that they are autobiographical: that is an illusion of Shakespeare's art.'[1]

Alas, if we took this advice, we would be marginalising the human interest and imposing a conventional allegorical pattern which would demean the strikingly unconventional and complex personal story told in the sonnets. The Professor's proposed allegory won't work anyway, given that his 'idealizing and spiritual' figure is likened by Shakespeare to 'lilies that fester', being a 'lascivious grace, in whom all ill well shows'.

The story told in the sequence is too *strange* to be fictional: indeed, you couldn't make it up. Certainly, a few of the sonnets may be relatively impersonal, notably the last two, with their conceits about Cupid's torch, which derive from verses by Marianus and resemble exercises in paradox (though even these, as we shall see, bear thematic relevance). The vast majority of the sonnets, however, ring true to personal experience. Indeed, some appear so intimately autobiographical as to be almost embarrassing to read: e.g. 42 and 137, and particularly 151, on 'conscience', with its outrageous French punning. In 42, the poet seeks (by sophistry) to console himself for the fact that his lady-love and the young man are copulating; and in 137 he laments his infatuation with a woman who is 'foul', 'a common place' and 'this false plague'. As for 151, 'Love is too young to know what conscience is': this makes sense only if we recall that *con* is French for 'cunt', so that 'conscience' can mean 'cunt-knowledge'. Other sonnets are characterised by what I term 'the opacity of the private': they hold that obscurity of allusion which characterises items written not for the public but primarily for the real person addressed. Examples include 107, 112, 117, and 125 – *whose canopy was borne by the poet?*

A sceptic could argue that in writing a sequence of amatory sonnets, Shakespeare was merely following the fashion established by Sir Philip Sidney's *Astrophel and Stella*, which was posthumously and influentially published in 1591. Indeed, that sceptic could even allege that Shakespeare's sonnets on the theme 'black is beautiful' (e.g. 127 and 132) seek to emulate Sidney's 7th sonnet, which enquires 'When Nature made her chief work, Stella's eyes, / In colour black why wrapt she beams so bright?'.

But this argument rapidly rebounds.

Most of Sidney's sonnets sound autobiographical. For instance, several bewail the fact that the woman he loves has a husband who is 'Rich'; and biographers confirm that Sidney's love, Penelope ('Stella') Devereux, was unhappily married to Robert, Lord Rich. In sonnet 28, Sidney even condemns proleptically Professor Bate's advice, by warning commentators not to apply 'Allegory's curious frame' to his sequence: the poet affirms 'When I say Stella, I do mean the same / Princess of beauty'. In other words, 'Don't you dare allegorise away into abstractions my real love for this real beautiful woman!' Again, in Edmund Spenser's *Amoretti* sequence (1595), we follow the courtship of an Elizabeth; sonnet 30 puns on Boyle; and Spenser indeed courted and married an Elizabeth Boyle. In short, contextual evidence suggests the likelihood that Shakespeare's sonnets, too, are strongly autobiographical. And so we find.

Will Shakespeare is present by name: he repeatedly puns on the name 'Will' – which also connotes wilful desire (sexual lust), carnal voracity, and the modern 'willy' (penis): see 135, 136 and 143. His wife, Anne *née* Hathaway, is punningly present ('And...hate away') in sonnet 145, which may have been the earliest to be composed. When talking of his often anguished relationship with the 'dark lady',

Shakespeare, being thereby an adulterer, refers to himself as a 'sinful' 'forsworn' lover (142, 152).

As for the 'lovely Boy': the evidence that he was the Earl of Southampton, Henry Wriothesley, born in 1573, varies from the weak to the strong. Weak?: 1. His initials, reversed, are those of the apparent dedicatee of the sonnets ('W.H.'). 2. In sonnet 20 (about the 'master-mistress', with craftily apt *feminine* rhyme-endings), we find the odd wording: 'a man in hew, all *Hews* in his controlling'. Though '*Hews*' ('appearances') suggests 'Hughes' or the plural 'Hughs' to some readers, to others it may suggest a crafty compression of the phrase 'He, Henry, leads W. S. (William Shakespeare)', and to yet others an acronym comprising the initials of 'Henry, Earle Wriothesley, of Southampton'. Strong evidence?: 1. The Earl was the patron to whom Shakespeare dedicated *Venus and Adonis* and – this time offering 'love...without end' – *The Rape of Lucrece*. 2. Portraits of the Earl depict a long-haired, decadent-looking and facially-feminine person: indeed, the Cobbe portrait of him was, for a long time, wrongly identified as that of a woman, Lady Norton. In that respect, it could be deemed a remarkably fitting likeness of the beloved young man with 'a woman's face'. Another candidate for the rôle of 'W.H.' (which by now suggests 'Who He?') is, of course, William Herbert, Earl of Pembroke, dedicatee of the First Folio, who, at the coronation of James I, 'actually kissed his Majesty's face, whereupon the King laughed and gave him a little cuff' (according to Giovanni Scaramelli, who was there); but Herbert, born in 1580, is probably too young for the rôle.

Above all, the story narrated in the sequence is strikingly unusual. Shakespeare evidently had a knack of getting himself into the sexual 'hot water' literalised in those two concluding sonnets – in which the stream, instead of extinguishing the blazing torch of desire, is heated by it. So perhaps that pair is more personal than it first seems.

As a lover, Shakespeare was *the Laureate of Sod's Law*. He reminds us that he is married (and we may recall that his spouse was pregnant at the time of the wedding), while elaborately recording his multiple infidelities. Evidently hired to persuade a young nobleman to marry and produce offspring, he initially complies with his instructions, but then falls in love with the man, and soon the poet is saying, in effect, 'Don't worry about not having children, for you will be immortalised in my verse. My poetry, instead of any offspring, will ensure that you live on for posterity.' The effeminate man is variously loving, critical, remote, decadent and treacherous. The poet then becomes sexually infatuated with a dark lady ('dark' as she is both black-haired and morally shady – 'dark as night'), but is racked by knowing that by conventional standards she lacks beauty, and furthermore she is promiscuous – 'the bay where all men ride'. Then, in a complication to delight novelists or film-makers, that man, who has been denounced as 'lascivious', actually becomes a lover of this woman. A contorted torment: our poet experiences a tantalising homoerotic relationship with a duplicitous nobleman who then fornicates with the courtesan who is the poet's mistress. No wonder Shakespeare sounds anguished; no wonder he produces not only 'Th'expense of spirit in a waste of shame' (punningly connoting the ejection of semen into a shameful vagina), but also 'Poor soul, the centre of my sinful earth'; her vagina is a seductive hell-hole (144, 129), and she is a 'plague' (137, 141). To confirm that the protagonist of the sonnets should indeed be called Shakespeare, sonnets 110 and 111 refer bitterly to his theatrical career, in which, on stage, he has been obliged to make himself 'a motley to the view', 'public means' engendering 'public manners'.

In short, to treat the sonnet sequence as impersonal ('a kind of exercise', suggests Bate) is a naïvely self-denying ordinance. You lose far more than you gain; your blinkered reading abjures much pleasure, understanding and emotional empathy. Furthermore, the complicated moral and emotional entanglements recorded in the sonnets are clearly driving Shakespeare towards the complexity of his mature dramatic writing. Crucial evidence comes in *Love's Labour's Lost*, where that 'black is beautiful' argument is incorporated and comically challenged ('To look like her are chimney-sweepers black'); and where, incongruously, Berowne's ferocious denunciation of Rosaline ('one that will do the deed / Though Argus were her eunuch and her guard') fits

Shakespeare's dark lady much better than the play's relatively innocent black-haired noblewoman: there private anguish distorts the public drama. The sonnets also anticipate *The Merchant of Venice* (frustrated love of an older man for a younger) and *Measure for Measure* (the sexual disgust and the portrayal of Angelo's hypocrisy). Cordelia's costly reticence in *King Lear*, Act I, is anticipated in sonnets 21, 23, 32, 84 and 85. Above all, the sexual treacheries described in the sonnets herald the intimate intensity of the depiction of jealousy in *Othello* and *The Winter's Tale*.

Roland Barthes's famous essay, 'The Death of the Author' (1968), scared numerous academics away from biographical approaches to literature – approaches which the essay appeared to prohibit. Those credulous readers overlooked the ironic intent. Barthes, a biographer who signed his works and claimed copyright, was accordingly *satirising* the stale notion that the author should be disregarded. Even Professor Bate, while warning us not to employ the biographical approach, confesses to having employed it himself – and most enjoyable were his results.

In the *Sonnets*, Shakespeare strove to confer durability and an epitomising magic on real people, relationships and emotions. There, the poet, who defiantly declares 'I am that I am', depicts not 'dramatic devices' but complex human beings who 'pace forth' down the centuries.

Note:
1. Jonathan Bate: 'Is This the Story of the Bard's Heart?': *The Times*, 20 April 2009, section 2, p. 14; and 'Shakespeare's Sonnets@400' on the Warwick University website. Incidentally, although some commentators have deemed the very spelling of the Bard's name a puzzle (for it appeared in diverse forms in his lifetime), I preserve the traditional spelling 'Shakespeare', for that is how it appears in the dedications of *Venus and Adonis* and *The Rape of Lucrece* and in the First Folio. It thereby gains sufficient authority.

3

The Taming of the Shrew: Why is It Allowed?

Here's an obvious puzzle for our times: why on earth is *The Taming of the Shrew* allowed to be shown? It's hard to imagine a play which is more demeaning to women, or which is more outrageously male-chauvinistic. Compared with Shakespeare in this play, Jeremy Clarkson is a *Guardian*-reading blue-stocking.

There's no way round it. From the start, the hero, Petruchio, is introduced as a selfish, mercenary fortune-hunter, who values a woman primarily for the wealth she should bring him. Of course, he also welcomes sexual gratification, and for that a woman must be the willing contributor. Kate (Katherina) displays resistance: very well, Kate must be 'tamed' like an animal, and at length, so she is, thoroughly. And the method of the taming? Abuse, physical and mental. Torture, psychological, prolonged. Eventually Kate is broken, and submits, making that long, humiliated and humiliating speech, declaring that a woman should be delighted to be the subject and servant of her husband:

> Such duty as the subject owes the prince,
> Even such a woman oweth to her husband.
> And when she is fróward, peevish, sullen, sour,
> And not obedient to his honest will,
> What is she but a foul contending rebel
> And graceless traitor to her loving lord? [...]
> Then vail your stomachs, for it is no boot,
> And place your hands below your husband's foot...[1]

Incredibly, texts of this grossly masculist play are allowed to be on sale, to be on open display, and even to be available in school libraries; and the drama is actually performed before audiences which include young impressionable boys and girls. Corrupt and corrupting, it blatantly celebrates masculine violence against women.

That's what can be said against it.

The only thing to be said *for* it is that it is also the most feminist play that Shakespeare ever wrote.

How can this claim be justified?

Easily. Think about the early circumstances. In the original Shakespearian productions, all the female parts were taken by males. See how this fact transforms it. That climactic speech about women accepting the rule of their lords – it didn't have the authority that a woman might give it. The speech was uttered by a boy or a high-voiced man. It was a joke. It was like, in recent times, a proposal of marriage from a pantomime dame to a handsome lad: the audience shares the gag. In a farce today, if an English actor were to play a Frenchman who declares that all Englishmen constitute a master-race, nobody in the audience would be so dim-witted as to take the claim seriously. We make due allowances. Indeed, in the case of that part of *The Taming of the Shrew*, it's the audience's knowledge that a male is speaking that turns the speech into a long joke appropriate to the whole gross tub-thumping comedy. Admittedly, in most of the other plays by Shakespeare, it is evident that we are indeed meant to suspend disbelief in female characters and to see them as thoroughly and credibly female: Cleopatra is an obvious example. So, what makes *The Taming of the Shrew* an exception to this rule? Answer: the first scene. In *The Taming of the Shrew*, the opening scene has told us of the elaborate attempt to deceive Christopher Sly, when, a lord explains,

> the boy will well usurp the grace,
> Voice, gait and action of a gentlewoman:
> I long to hear him call the drunkard 'husband'...

Therefore, in this comedy, from the outset, we are thoroughly alerted to the convention by which the male actor pretends to be female.

But what can you do to redeem the play these days, when it is not customary for women's parts to be played by males? The answer is obvious. Indeed, the answer was acted out splendidly at the Globe some time ago. That was in an *all-female* production. Janet McTeer played Petruchio to Kathryn Hunter's Kate. As McTeer's Petruchio swaggered, blustered and bullied (and even urinated against a pillar – I feared being splashed), the effect was to make the play a satire on aggressive *machismo*. In that production, as the long climactic 'submission' speech was performed, it provoked dawning dismay from the supposedly male listeners on stage, while Kate became increasingly delighted by the power of her own eloquence. Their initially approving nods and sentimental tears gave way to consternation and alarm. If you thought of those hearers as *male* characters, you could infer that they were dismayed by the sheer rhetorical power of the female, whose apparent advocacy of submission was subverted by her evident oratorical dominance. If you thought of them as *females posing as male*, the dismay could be construed as that of females feeling increasingly betrayed by the arguments thus deployed by a woman against women.

And there are umpteen other ways in which, in productions, that speech can be redeemed. If the performer is female, one way is to let her give a knowing wink as she speaks, to indicate that the speech is merely ironic and not to be taken literally. (Mary Pickford did this in a 1929 film version.) Another way is to let the speaker appear to be deranged, a victim beaten into neurotic or psychotic submission by her brutal treatment. (A production by Charles Marowitz in the 1970s featured a raped and deranged Kate.)

But, in my view, no way is better than to let the play be performed by an all-female cast, making the whole drama a satire on chauvinistic masculinity. And that way is historically the most appropriate too, for it is culturally symmetrical with that procedure of Shakespeare's day, whereby the female roles were usually performed by males.

Of course, there will always be some pessimistic reactionary among us who will say: 'What is the point of trying to make Shakespeare politically and ethically congenial to our age? Can't we simply accept the obvious, which is that he lived four hundred years ago and necessarily reflected the values of his times, values which are now out of date? You can't make a silk purse out of a sow's ear, and you can't turn Shakespeare into a feminist.'

To which there are many answers, but a cogent answer is provided by Emilia in Othello:

>   Let husbands know
> Their wives have sense like them: they see, and smell,
> And have their palates both for sweet and sour,
> As husbands have. [...]
>   And have not we affections,
> Desires for sport, and frailty, as men have?
> Then let them use us well; else let them know,
> The ills we do, their ills instruct us so.

This shows not only that feminist ideas were available to Shakespeare, but also that he could voice them incisively. It is to a great feminist of recent times, Germaine Greer, that we owe some of the most sympathetic accounts of Shakespeare. Indeed, in one of her books (*Shakespeare*, 1986) she argued that women owe Shakespeare an immense historical debt for having propagated so radiantly and influentially the notion that marriage should be based not on the dominance of the male or the submission of the female but on loving mutuality.

So perhaps the ideal production of *The Taming of the Shrew* would be one directed jointly by Germaine Greer and Emilia. To be fair, it should alternate with a version directed by Jeremy Clarkson and Iago, who are no strangers to irony.

Note:
1. Citations from *The Taming of the Shrew* and *Othello* are from the Wordsworth Classics' editions by Cedric Watts (dated 2004 and 2001 respectively).

4

What is the Plot of *Love's Labour's Won*? – or, Seeing the Invisible.

Puzzle: how can we see an invisible play? G. R Hibbard, editing *Love's Labour's Lost* for Oxford University Press (1998), notes that *Love's Labour's Won* existed, was published, and disappeared. He concludes: 'Further than that it is not possible to go.' Here, I claim that it is possible to go *much* further. Indeed, what we know of *Love's Labour's Won* is already sufficient to transform *Love's Labour's Lost*.

In 1598, when Francis Meres listed in his *Palladis Tamia* the plays by Shakespeare that he knew, he included among the excellent comedies 'his *Loue labors lost*, his *Loue labours wonne*'. This created a puzzle for scholars, as no work entitled *Love's Labour's Won* (as '*Loue labours wonne*' is customarily modernised) had survived. Some scholars speculated that it might simply be an alternative title of one of the extant comedies not named by Meres, probably *The Taming of the Shrew*, possibly *Much Ado about Nothing* or *All's Well That Ends Well*. (Leslie Hotson even proposed *Troilus and Cressida*.) But, in 1953, an old fragment of a bookseller's list was found. That fragment, dated 1603, listed 'loves labor lost' and 'loves labor won', as well as 'taming of a shrew'. This appeared to confirm that *Love's Labour's Won* (evidently not *The Taming of the Shrew* with a different title) was indeed a lost comedy by Shakespeare. Significantly, both Meres and the bookseller place its title *immediately after* that of *Love's Labour's Lost*; and Meres confirms that the play had appeared by 1598. The First Quarto of *Titus Andronicus* vanished utterly – until, amazingly, a single copy appeared in Sweden in 1904; so perhaps *Love's Labour's Won* will fully materialise as a quarto one day.

We should now recall what was so odd and original about *Love's Labour's Lost*. As Berowne says there, 'Our wooing doth not end like an old play: / Jack hath not Jill.' What made that comedy so brilliantly open-ended and so strikingly feminist a work was that the women, after repeatedly outwitting the men, finally did not accept prompt nuptials but insisted that marriage be deferred and be conditional on good conduct by the males. In retrospect, we can now understand this unconventionality. The remarkable open-endedness of *Love's Labour's Lost*, with its frequent invocations of the future, was designed to solicit the joyful multiple *closure* provided by *Love's Labour's Won*.

What happens in *Love's Labour's Won* is evidently this. After the year of waiting which the ladies had stipulated, the King and the three lords meet again and compare experiences. Each concedes that he has failed to be as diligently faithful and austere as he had been enjoined by his lady to be. (You can tell that from the way they behave in *Love's Labour's Lost*, where they break pledges and are inconsistent.) Each, again, seeks to conceal his failings and impress the ladies. Those ladies, whose own conduct has not been totally above reproach, once again outwit and humiliate the men. (The outwitting is achieved by further eavesdropping. A standard device of Shakespearian comedy, it had been employed exuberantly and self-parodically in *Love's Labour's Lost*.) Nevertheless, after these comical complications, all is forgiven, and the long-deferred wedding celebrations provide the culmination of the play. Jack does, after all, have Jill. The same rustic characters, Costard and company, enliven the action, and once again they perform a farcical play-within-the-play. This time, as appropriate accompaniment to the nuptials, the rustics ludicrously adapt a famous Ovidian legend of love: a linkage which will recur later, in *A Midsummer Night's Dream*. Next, Armado weds Jaquenetta, his three-year probation having been reduced to one year, as her child needs a guaranteed bread-winning father. The rustics then provide a concluding song about love, marriage and the seasonal cycle, as they had previously done, once again warning hearers of the risk of cuckoldry for the husband.

All this is obvious, when you think about it. Indeed, if you combine the characters, some situations and the openness of *Love's*

Labour's Lost with what they clearly portend (and with parts of the plot of *A Midsummer Night's Dream*), it's quite possible to stage *Love's Labour's Won* in the theatre of your imagination. When you stage it there, you may find that at times it is as entertaining as its 'prequel'; for it is enlivened by the alternations of resonantly lyrical poetry, erudite wit and farcical comedy. It is marred only by the obsessively-recurrent gags about horns and horning, harts and hearts, French crowns and pox.

Shakespeare, at this stage in his development as a playwright, was fascinated by degrees of open-endedness, and by ironic parallels between earlier and later plays. His second history tetralogy, and particularly the relationship between Parts 1 and 2 of *Henry IV*, come to mind. In those two history dramas, characters and a play-within-a-play recur. Throughout that tetralogy, a sequence of partly-open endings anticipates a sequence of partial closures; and eventually the Epilogue of *Henry V* turns the sequence into a cycle. So *Love's Labour's Lost* and *Love's Labour Won* together relate well to the structural preoccupations of that period, 1594-99. Shakespeare is preoccupied by what I have termed elsewhere (selecting from 'silken terms precise') 'transtextual narratives': typically, plots which extend across two or more works, generating prospective and retrospective ironies.

Of course, the presence of *Love's Labour's Won* does seem to blunt the radicalism of its predecessor. It shows that Shakespeare's brilliant comedy of feminism, *Love's Labour's Lost*, was largely an experimental feint before its sequel's reassertion of matrimony and patriarchal order. But then, as we noted in the previous chapter, in her book entitled *Shakespeare*, Germaine Greer, no less, has asserted that Shakespeare's advocacy of heterosexual love culminating in matrimony was his most progressive and influential cultural achievement. 'He projected the ideal so luminously.'

By the way, you'll already have spotted a titular puzzle. Scholars conventionally use the form *'Love's Labour's Won'* because that makes a symmetrical counterpart to *'Love's Labour's Lost'*. Both titles, however, are obviously illogical. We'll disentangle that puzzle in the following chapter.

The first leaf of *Love's Labour's Won*, with its witty dialogue between Moth and Armado, has been published; though, sadly, the rest was destroyed by fire. These events, however, occurred in the realm of fiction: in *Love Lies Bleeding* (1948), a detective novel by 'Edmund Crispin' (the pseudonym of Bruce Montgomery). Given that *Love's Labour's Won* would, like *Love's Labour's Lost*, have played with planes of reality and illusion, its brief resurrection and destruction *in a novel* provide an entirely appropriate tribute. (The tribute is augmented by recent comedies with similar titles, written by David Fanstone and Ryan Smith.) We then recognise that postmodernism was thriving for centuries before, among other 'figures pedantical', the term 'postmodernism' was invented for it by some latter-day Armado or Holofernes.

5

Love's Labour's Lost: An Illogical Title?

Love's Labour's Lost: that's how the title is traditionally presented by editors, and that's how I usually present it in this book, lest I be deemed guilty of ignoring misprints. But *Love's Labour's Lost* is very odd, isn't it? An apostrophe appears not only in *'Love's'* but also in *'Labour's'*. Every editor seems to put it like that: certainly Peter Alexander in the collection published by Collins; G. Blakemore Evans *et al.* for *The Riverside Shakespeare*; Wells and Taylor for the Oxford *Complete Works*, G. R Hibbard for Oxford World's Classics; and Richard David and H. R. Woudhuysen for Arden: to mention only a sample. It's the standard rendering. But that second apostrophe makes little sense. The sooner it goes, the better!

The meaning of the traditionally-edited title is thus: 'The labour of love is lost', or, more clearly, 'The endeavour of love is wasted', which could refer very loosely to the fact that the play's male lovers are denied speedy marriage by their ladies and must frustratedly wait for a year (or three years, in the case of Armado). That meaning is a *very* loose fit, because the men can live in hope; they have not been rejected but are only on probation, so to speak; and therefore their endeavours as wooers have not really been wasted. As I shall demonstrate, a far better spelling, being more logical and more harmonious with the context, would be thus: *Love's Labours Lost*; and that's how I'll give it subsequently in this chapter, unless I'm deliberately citing the traditional version. The absence of one apostrophe can make a great deal of difference; in this case, a harmonising difference.

In the earliest text, the title lacked any apostrophes, and thereby created a teasing ambiguity. That first Quarto (Q1) has simply *'Loues labors lost'*. It looks quite proleptic, anticipating that slothfully uncouth elimination of apostrophes which nowadays is a burgeoning

21

vice. (Proper nouns and place-names suffer particularly, these days: 'King's Cross', for instance, often becomes 'Kings Cross' and even 'Kingscross'; though greengrocers, notoriously, as if to compensate, find new homes for the exiled signs by industriously creating such plurals as 'apple's' and 'plum's'.) The First Folio of 1623 (F1) started the play's false titular tradition by introducing one apostrophe: *'Loves Labour's Lost'*. This text was set from Q1, and introduced many corrections and many new errors. That apostrophe, I submit, is one of the new errors. For us, the resultant puzzle hinges partly on the ambiguity of *'Lost'*, which could mean 'wasted' or 'failed to gain (some object)'.

'Our wooing doth not end like an old play: / Jack hath not Jill', says the bemused Berowne when *Love's Labours Lost* is hastening towards its unconventional ending. (Though some editors call him 'Biron', Q1 and F1 specify 'Berowne'.) Unexpectedly and remarkably, this romantic comedy does not end with the multiple marriages which we expect, and which occur in *The Taming of the Shrew*, *The Two Gentlemen of Verona*, *A Midsummer Night's Dream*, *As You Like It* and *The Merchant of Venice*, for example. So, as we have seen, *Love's Labours Lost* can seem a remarkably feminist play. Its women are generally more intelligent and practical than their men; and, eventually, instead of settling for speedy marriage, they are shrewd in setting those terms of probation for their wooers. However, as I argued in the previous chapter, Shakespeare envisaged *Love's Labours Lost* as the first play of a pair: its 'open ends' invite and herald the closures provided by its sequel.

Shakespeare, from the outset of his career, had kept his eye on the ways in which a play might generate successors, sequels or even 'prequels': the *Henry VI trilogy* suggests this. Later, the open-ended features of *Richard II* prepare us for the partial closures in *1 Henry IV*, and that play clearly points to events to be portrayed in *2 Henry IV*, which in turn explicitly solicits *Henry V*. We know that *Antony and Cleopatra* provides an intricately ironic commentary on *Julius Caesar*; that *Troilus and Cressida* often resembles a cynical riposte to *Romeo and Juliet*, and that the depiction of the tragic Othello looks like cultural compensation for the depiction of a previous Moor, the lustfully Machiavellian Aaron in *Titus Andronicus*. Shakespeare often thought dialectically. One work would engender the contrast and continuity provided by another. Typically, in the *Sonnets*, loving and reproachful addresses to a man are followed by loving and reproachful addresses to a woman. The great tragedies are balanced by the late Romances. In *Othello*, Iago swears 'by Janus' (the two-faced god, who looks in opposite directions at the same time); sometimes Shakespeare may have sworn by that deity too. That is one of the claims pervading this book

As we have seen, when Francis Meres (in his *Palladis Tamia*, 1598) listed Shakespeare's comedies, the entry '*Loue labors lost*' was followed immediately by '*Loue labours wonne*'; and Christopher Hunt in August 1603 included in his list '*loves labor lost, loves labor won*'. So *Love's Labours Lost* was the first of a pair of Shakespearian comedies, its action being concluded in a sequel, *Love's Labours Won*, which surely would end happily with the four postponed marriages.

So how should that second play's title appear today? Obviously, as I have specified above, as *Love's Labours Won,* meaning 'The endeavours of love did (on this occasion) win the prize of matrimony'. But, since that is the case, the preceding play should be titularly harmonious, symmetrical with its partner, and should bear not the customary title *Love's Labour's Lost* (intransitively meaning 'The endeavour of love is wasted') but, instead, the title *Love's Labours Lost,* bearing the harmoniously transitive significance, 'The endeavours of love failed to win the prize of matrimony'. Obviously, *Love's Labours Won* cannot mean merely 'Love's labours acquired (or were acquired)', for that would be grammatically incomplete. As it cannot, that excludes retrospectively the corresponding meaning 'Love's labours abandoned or wasted (or were wasted)' for *Love's Labours Lost.*

In any case, the plural '*Labours*', rather than the singular '*Labour's*' or Hunt's singular *Labor*, is clearly appropriate to a pair of works which feature ironically-interwoven wooing by no fewer than five men: the French King, three courtiers, and Armado. If the word's connotations also include the legendary labours of Hercules, that would be appropriate, given that, in the earlier of the two plays, Hercules appears as a character performed by Moth (or Mote); and furthermore, if the connotations include the labours of childbirth, that would fit Jaquenetta. She doubtless would have experienced that ordeal in the time-span between the earlier play, in which she is pregnant, and the later play, in which, as the action must occur a year or so later (when the probationary periods are over), she will be a mother, and will fulfil the undertaking to marry Armado to ensure a fatherly wage-earning presence. (We and Costard may, however, doubt Armado's paternity of the child. In the earlier of the two plays, there were good clues to indicate that crafty Costard, the effective inseminator, had fooled gullible Armado.) The entry of that new life, Jaquenetta's baby, will aptly compensate for the previous comedy's famously dramatic incursion of death, proclaimed (aptly) by Lamord, whose name sounds like 'La Mort'.

In short, Q1's *'labors'*, lacking an apostrophe, is preferable to F1's *'Labour's'*. Preserving the Q1 version will save time, ink and money; and Occam's razor (shaving superfluity) incisively confirms my choice. Tradition should defer to logic; and just as Juliet's illogical 'O Romeo, Romeo, wherefore art thou Romeo?' should one day be superseded by the logical 'O Romeo Mountague, wherefore art thou "Mountague"?', so the traditional title *Love's Labour's Lost* should eventually be superseded by the rational and labour-saving *Love's Labours Lost* (ideally with a seemingly-Americanised but authentic spelling – *Labors* instead of *Labours*). In *A Midsummer Night's Dream*, Quince's ignorant neglect of punctuation farcically renders 'all disordered' the prologue that he utters: which proves that Shakespeare would appreciate and applaud our respectful attention to apostrophes here. As Quince proves, this is a matter not of pedantry but of communication; not of the limited but of the extensive.

Indeed, a detail of punctuation can be a matter of life or death: in Christopher Marlowe's *Edward II*,[1] a mere comma seals the fate of the King himself. In that play, Mortimer Junior is pleased with an ambiguous letter bearing the Latin injunction 'Edwardum occidere nolite timere bonum est'. If the reader mentally adds a comma after 'timere', it means 'Fear not to kill the king, 'tis good he die'; but if the comma is added after 'nolite', it means 'Kill not the king, 'tis good to fear the worst'. Thus Mortimer hopes to decree the murder while appearing not to. In the event, both Edward II and Mortimer are slain. Latin saved the life of Ben Jonson, but it brought them no favours.

6

Why do Romeo and the Friar Utter the Same Speech?
The Puzzle of the Address to 'grey eyde morne' in *Romeo and Juliet.*

In *Discoveries*, Ben Jonson famously grumbled that Shakespeare 'never blotted out line', commenting: 'Would he had blotted a thousand.'[1] Jonson held that Shakespeare wrote all too fluently and (therefore) carelessly. But there is plenty of evidence that Shakespeare did indeed 'blot out line': he often deleted and replaced material. The numerous differences between, for instance, the Quarto and Folio versions of *King Lear* show this. On some occasions, though, he either failed to cancel a passage which he meant to delete, or failed to make clear to others that a passage should be deleted. Editors are then obliged to become amateur detectives.

Consider *Love's Labour's Lost*. (Deferring modestly to tradition, I revert to conventional punctuation of that title.) In what is now Act 4, scene 3, we find two versions of the same speech about the inspiration provided by the 'Promethean fire' of women's eyes. The second version is the lengthier and is generally better. In addition, in Act 5, scene 2, Rosaline's stipulation that Berowne must spend time helping the sick appears in a very brief version and in a longer, fully developed version. A stranger instance of duplication confronts editors in *Julius Cæsar*, in Act 4, scene 2. There the death of Portia, Brutus's wife, is announced not once but twice, and on the second occasion Brutus responds in a strikingly different way. It looks as if Shakespeare tried two methods of handling this poignant event, but both sequences instead have survived when only one should have done. Perhaps, writing in haste, he forgot to cancel, or failed to cancel clearly, the version he deemed inferior; or – a third option – perhaps he simply could not make up his mind. A decision would then have been made in the theatre, but that has gone unrecorded. (I return to this matter in a later chapter.)

In *Romeo and Juliet*, we encounter a related textual problem: a duplicated speech, given to two speakers. The earliest texts of the play are the First Quarto (Q1) and the Second Quarto (Q2). The former may derive from actors' recollections of stage productions; and the latter (which is longer and often of higher quality) is widely regarded as more authoritative. The evidence that Q2 derives largely from Shakespeare's own draft is convincing enough. One piece of evidence is the presence of loose or 'permissive' stage-directions (e.g. '*Enter three or foure Citizens*'), usually deemed by scholars to indicate the presence of a playwright who couldn't be troubled to work out the logistics in detail as he initially composed the work. Another piece of evidence is that at what is now 4.5.99, we find, instead of '*Enter Seruingman*' or '*Enter Peter*', the direction '*Enter Will Kemp*', a reference to the leading comic actor in Shakespeare's company.[2]

The problem of duplication emerges at the end of Act 2, scene 2, and at the beginning of Act 2, scene 3. (I use present-day Act and scene references.) First, here is the version offered by Q2:

> *Ro.* I would I were thy bird.
> *Ju*: Sweete so would I,
> Yet I should kill thee with much cherishing:
> Good night, good night.
> Parting is such sweete sorrow,
> That I shall say good night, till it be morrow.
>   *Ju.* Sleepe dwel vpon thine eyes, peace in thy breast.
>   *Ro.* Would I were sleepe and peace so sweet to rest,
> The grey eyde morne smiles on the frowning night,
> Checkring the Easterne Clouds with streaks of light
> And darknesse fleckted like a drunkard reeles,
> From forth daies pathway, made by *Tytans* wheeles.
> Hence will I to my ghostly Friers close cell,
> His helpe to crave, and my deare hap to tell.
>   *Exit.*
> *Enter Frier alone with a basket.*   (night,
>   *Fri.* The grey-eyed morne smiles on the frowning
> Checking the Easterne clowdes with streaks of light:

And fleckeld darknesse like a drunkard reeles,
From forth daies path, and *Titans* burning wheeles:
Now ere the sun aduance his burning eie,
The day to cheere, and nights dancke dewe to drie,
I must vpfill this osier cage of ours,
With balefull weedes, and precious iuyced flowers [etc....]

Now, here is the version offered by an Arden edition. In this case, the square brackets are those furnished by that version.

Romeo. I would I were thy bird.
Juliet.   Sweet, so would I:
Yet I should kill thee with much cherishing.
 Good night, good night. Parting is such sweet sorrow
That I shall say good night till it be morrow.   185
                                        [*Exit Juliet.*]
Romeo. Sleep dwell upon thine eyes, peace in thy breast.
 Would I were sleep and peace so sweet to rest.
The grey-ey'd morn smiles on the frowning night,
Chequering the eastern clouds with streaks of light;
And darkness fleckled like a drunkard reels   190
From forth day's pathway, made by Titan's wheels.
Hence will I to my ghostly Sire's close cell,
His help to crave and my dear hap to tell.   [*Exit.*]

[SCENE III]

Enter FRIAR [LAURENCE] *alone with a basket.*

Friar L. Now, ere the sun advance his burning eye
The day to cheer, and night's dank dew to dry,
I must upfill this osier cage of ours
With baleful weeds and precious-juiced flowers.[2]

Although editors generally regard Q2 as superior to Q1, an Arden editor, Brian Gibbons, here chose to follow Q1 when allocating his line 186 to Romeo instead of Juliet. The main problem is conspicuous. Q2 is clearly faulty in ascribing both to Romeo and to

28

the Friar the four lines (numbered 188-91 by Arden, above) describing the dawn. You can't let both of them speak the lines. If you did, then, in the theatre, it would sound as if one of the actors had mistakenly learnt a passage that belonged to the other fellow, or as if the second actor had forgotten his own stuff and was parroting what he had just heard – anticipating the hypnotic ventriloquism of Strindberg's *Miss Julie*.

Thus, whether these four lines about dawn should be given to Romeo or to the Friar is mainly a matter of critical judgement, particularly judgement of their appropriateness to the speaker. That Arden editor decided that 'the lines are characteristic of Romeo rather than the uninventive personifications of the Friar'; so he allocated the passage to Romeo. Yet both Q1 and Q2 give these lines to the Friar. Q2's additional ascription of them to Romeo may be the compositor's erring allocation of some marginal rewriting by Shakespeare. Therefore, the reader may be inclined to think that the Friar should (by two textual 'votes' to one) be allowed these few moments of inventiveness.

You can probably see another reason for favouring the Friar. If the passage is given to Romeo (as it was by Gibbons), the transition from line 187 to line 188 is oddly abrupt. What's more, the tone is surely wrong. Romeo has just spent a rapturous time with Juliet (he has learnt that she reciprocates his feelings of love), so he has good grounds for thinking of that night as 'smiling' rather than 'frowning'. He should sound gratified and resolute. If, on the other hand, they are given to the Friar, those four lines about daybreak blend naturally with the following couplet about dew at dawn. As he explains, the dewy daybreak is the appropriate time for him to be gathering weeds and flowers. Being an early-rising botanist, he naturally takes an interest in the weather that prevails as he walks the fields. Problem solved, I submit.

I take encouragement from the fact that, although that Arden edition ascribes the passage to Romeo's speech at the end of scene 2, other important editions (such as the *Riverside* and the Norton) have ascribed it to the Friar's speech at the beginning of scene 3. What at first appears to be a simple scholarly matter is clearly also a critical matter, concerning the aptness of a speech for a given character at a given time. In this case, the allocation, once made, modifies two characters. Another lesson is that if we compare a modern edition with a reprint of the early text, we usually have surprises. Editing is never innocent but is constantly reshaping the early materials so as to transform them in the way that the editor finds most congenial.

Of course, the editor's endeavours may be counter-productive. What is textually congenial to one person may be uncongenial to another. An industrious scholar may unintentionally garble the script, though in performance it may be mended. Or, as the sententious Friar himself puts it:

> Virtue itself turns vice, being misapplied,
> And vice sometime's by action dignified.

Notes:
1. *Discoveries* in *Ben Jonson*, ed. C. H. Herford and Percy and Evelyn Simpson, Vol. 8 (London: Oxford U. P., 1947), p. 583.
2. *Romeo and* Juliet, ed. Brian Gibbon (London: Methuen, 1980; rpt., 1983). Unless otherwise specified, in this chapter the remaining references to *Romeo and Juliet* are to my edition (Ware: Wordsworth Editions, 2000).

7

Why does Juliet say 'Romeo' when she means 'Mountague'? (And why are the editors as illogical as Juliet?)

Juliet, though only thirteen years of age, is the most intelligent character in *Romeo and Juliet*. The more you study the text, the more evident that becomes. For instance: in the famous love-scene with Romeo, Act 2, scene 2, she takes the lead, firmly rebuking him for swearing by the moon (symbol of inconstancy), prophetically warning him of the rashness of their haste, and astutely steering his passionate wooing in the direction of holy matrimony.

This renders all the more peculiar what happens early in that scene, when she thinks she is alone. She blunders into illogicality. She does so in what has become the most famous line of the play – indeed, one of the dozen-or-so most famous lines in the whole of Shakespeare:

O Romeo, Romeo, wherefore art thou Romeo?[1]

'Wherefore', of course, means 'why', and she is saying, in effect,'O, why do you have to be afflicted with the name "Romeo"?'. But the line, as she thus utters it, is patently wrong. There is nothing obnoxious in the Christian name 'Romeo'. It's the *surname* that should worry her. What she should be saying is:

O Romeo Mountague, wherefore art thou Mountague?

– or, to be even more precise:

O Romeo Mountague, wherefore art thou 'Mountague'?

('Mountague', not 'Montague', is the usual spelling of that surname in the earliest texts, the first and second quartos.) Clearly, Juliet should be lamenting the fact that Romeo's surname, 'Mountague', shows that he belongs to the very clan with which her own clan, the Capulets', has been feuding long and violently. In loving a Mountague, she is loving a man from the family which her own parents detest. Since Juliet, in this famous line, makes so obvious a blunder, you would think that some kindly editors would by now have established in the text that correct version:

> O Romeo Mountague, wherefore art thou Mountague?

But they haven't. In text after text, edition after edition, nobody comes to Juliet's rescue.

Indeed, so familiar is the ostensibly erroneous line that some editors pass over it silently, without comment. Others make peripheral comments: for instance, by explaining that 'Wherefore' does not mean 'Where', or by claiming that both 'Romeo' and 'Juliet' may be pronounced disyllabically.

Even more strangely, some commentators have sought to defend the apparently indefensible by claiming that the line is logical as it stands. For example, the eminent American Professor, Stephen Orgel, claims that Juliet is correct in specifying not 'Montague' (which he prefers to 'Mountague') but 'Romeo'; and he argues thus:

> In fact, in a Renaissance index of names, we would be much more likely to find Romeo listed under 'Romeo' than under 'Montague'. For example, Halle's *Chronicle*, an essential source-book of modern English history for Shakespeare's age, indexes Anne Bulleyn under Anne, and Stephen Gardiner [*sic*] under Stephen.[2]

This scholarly defence is briskly defeated by the fact that Halle's index lists Anne Bulleyn as 'Anne Bulleyn' and Stephen Gardyner as 'Stephen Gardyner'. Therefore, in an index of this kind, 'Romeo' would *not* be severed from the surname. Consequently, if Juliet *had* followed Halle's example, she would indeed have said, 'O Romeo Mountague', as she should.

In contrast to Stephen Orgel, Professor Simon Palfrey, another redoubtably knowledgeable commentator, offers an *aesthetic* defence of the line. His argument is:

> 'Romeo' is so much more intimate to Juliet than 'Montague' could ever be. The sound of his name is beautiful to her, the more so in English with its adjacent sighs (oh) separated only by the personal pronoun (me). The relatively tinny and adult 'Montague' could not remotely perform this function.[3]

This fancifully appreciative argument is foiled by two facts. 1: Juliet there is ostensibly *deploring* (not relishing) the name 'Romeo': that's part of the problem. 2: The 'correct' version of the line would *also* contain 'Romeo'.

Thus, Orgel's citation of old-fashioned indexes and Palfrey's appeal to the auditory beauty of the name 'Romeo' both fail to provide cogent answers to the original charge, that Juliet is being conspicuously illogical. She is uttering, and treating as opprobrious, the Christian name 'Romeo', instead of the name which she clearly *intended* to utter and treat as opprobrious – the surname 'Mountague'. What makes the illogicality so conspicuous is the context, and particularly the passage which follows immediately after the problematic line. There she says:

> Deny thy father and refuse thy name;
> Or, if thou wilt not, be but sworn my love,
> And I'll no longer be a Capulet.

'Deny thy father' means 'Forsake your paternal surname, "Mountague".' She confirms this by saying that if he will not forsake it, she will solve the problem by ceasing to be (not Juliet, but) a Capulet. Already she is envisaging a time when she will be married to Romeo. So, in these words, she subverts the well-intentioned defences by Orgel and Palfrey. To make the matter utterly unambiguous, she proceeds to say:

> 'Tis but thy name that is my enemy.
> Thou art thyself, though not a Mountague.

O be some other name! What's Mountague?

Thus, Juliet herself abundantly confirms that she should indeed, logically, have said:

O Romeo Mountague, wherefore art thou Mountague?

Having thrown stones, I hear the tinkling of glass. My conscience now obliges me to confess that, when editing *Romeo and Juliet*, I presented the 'correct' line only in an endnote, while preserving the 'incorrect' line in the main text. There were, however, three reasons for this.

Reason 1. Cowardice and modesty overcame clarity and logic. Who am I, I thought, to change so drastically, in the main text, a line which, for centuries, has been found memorably attractive by so many people?

Reason 2. Juliet's error can be justified on the grounds of realistic psychology. In the manner of a 'Freudian slip', she is accidentally revealing her inner preoccupation with the notion, later explicit, that what should matter is the distinctive individual and not any label the individual bears: 'What's in a name?' – in *any* name? That old philosophical conundrum is preoccupying her, and she is astutely siding with the nominalists – descendants of Plato's Hermogenes. (In the Platonic dialogue *Cratylus*, Hermogenes claims that the relationship of names to entities is a matter of convention and not of natural identity. The proper noun 'Hermogenes', for instance, means 'son of Hermes', but Hermogenes himself lacks Hermes' good fortune.) Certainly, Shakespeare possessed the knowledge to let Juliet's words imply unconscious or subconscious thought-processes revealed by a slip: the proof is that Mercutio's Freudian 'Queen Mab' speech had exuberantly explained unconscious associations of ideas. Arguably, then, Juliet's illogicality has been logically designed.

Reason 3 is this. The 'error' may be an instance of symbolic prolepsis (anticipation) by Shakespeare. As the play has made clear, the name 'Romeo' means 'Pilgrim': that's why Romeo chose the guise of a pilgrim at the Capulet's ball, and why he repeatedly addresses Juliet as his 'saint'. And, predominantly, it is the exalted romantic conception of love as a religion, desire regarded as pilgrimage to a saint, which brings Romeo to his death, followed by Juliet. 'Romeo' is a name symbolising the idealistic but lethal potential of romantic love. So Juliet's error in logic reveals not only Shakespeare's psychological realism but also his symbolic accuracy. Probably the original line should stand, therefore, after all.

Notes:
1. 2.2.33. Textual citations from *Romeo and Juliet* are from the edition by Cedric Watts (Ware: Wordsworth Editions, 2000).
2. Stephen Orgel: 'Introduction' to John Sutherland and Cedric Watts: *Henry V, War Criminal? and Other Shakespeare Puzzles* (Oxford: Oxford U. P., 2000), p. xiv.
3. Simon Palfrey: *The Connell Guide to Shakespeare's 'Romeo and Juliet'* (Chippenham: Connell Guides, 2012), pp. 59-60.

8

Does Shakespeare Condemn Extra-Marital Copulation?

A reader of the magazine *Around the Globe*, while criticising in an email one of my puzzle-articles, firmly declared: 'Shakespeare does not go in for love outside of marriage.' As love, in Shakespeare's plays, often (of course) precedes marriage, the reader evidently meant to say: 'Shakespeare does not approve of extra-marital copulation.' But is this really the case? Is the Bard so restrictive?

The reader was thinking primarily of *Romeo and Juliet*. There, in Act 2, scene 2, when Romeo (anticipating Mick Jagger's famous lament) craves 'satisfaction', saying 'O wilt thou leave me so unsatisfied?', Juliet somewhat indignantly retorts: 'What satisfaction canst thou have tonight?'; and she then quickly steers his ardour in the direction of marriage. Although the *Oxford Companion to English Literature* asserts that *Romeo* takes the lead ('he...wins her consent to a secret marriage'), it is actually Juliet, mature beyond her thirteen years, who takes control of the amatory situation and deftly plans the speedy wedlock. We may also recall the words of Hermia in *A Midsummer Night's Dream*, Act 2, sc. 2. At night-time, Hermia insists that her wooer, Lysander, should lie further away from her: 'Such separation as may well be said / Becomes a virtuous bachelor and a maid.' Then there is Prospero's remarkably explicit speech (in *The Tempest*, Act 4, sc. 1) in which he warns Ferdinand not to violate Miranda's virginity before the wedding-day, otherwise

> barren hate,
> Sour-eyed disdain, and discord shall bestrew
> The union of your bed with weeds so loathly
> That you shall hate it both.[1]

Once again, Germaine Greer's comment (in her book *Shakespeare*) is apt:

> Shakespeare...projected the ideal of the monogamous heterosexual couple so luminously [in his writings] that they irradiate our notions of compatibility and co-operation between spouses to this day.

Shakespeare has indeed been a memorable propagandist for the notion that love between a man and a woman should properly culminate in wedlock. We may think not only of Romeo and Juliet or Ferdinand and Miranda, but also of Rosalind and Orlando or Florizel and Perdita.

Furthermore, numerous works associate extra-marital sexual intercourse with vice, corruption and disorder. Plays which appear to condemn such illicit sexuality include *Titus Andronicus*, in which the wicked Aaron copulates adulterously with Tamora, and *King Lear*, in which the blinding of Gloucester is directly related to his adulterous lust: 'The dark and vicious place where thee he got / Cost him his eyes', Edgar sternly informs the illegitimate Edmund. Clearly, Edmund's extra-marital entanglements with Regan and Goneril help to destroy him and them. In turn, *Troilus and Cressida* suggests that 'appetite' (whether the appetite for power or the appetite for illicit sexual gratification) is a 'universal wolf', creating disorder and destruction. The whole pointless war is caused by the adultery of Helen with Paris. 'All the argument is a cuckold and a whore', observes Thersites in the Quarto text; 'All the argument is a Whore and a Cuckold', echoes Thersites in the Folio. The love of Troilus and Cressida, consummated outside marriage, ends bitterly for Troilus.

One of the themes of this puzzle-book is that Shakespeare was often a Janiform writer. Like the god Janus, he is two-faced, able to look in opposite directions simultaneously. Shakespeare produced the most brilliant sequence of love-sonnets in literature, and those sonnets declare the poet's extra-marital, indeed adulterous, love for a woman. Even more to the point, many of the most poignant and memorable of the love-sonnets are addressed to the beautiful young man. As we have seen in Chapter 2, the majority of the sonnets read most naturally as poetically-intensified personal statements by

William Shakespeare: the narrative seems too unconventional to be invented. The sonnets show that the complexities of extra-marital love and sexuality render life sometimes ecstatic and sometimes bitter, but always vivid. Our poet evidently experienced to the full a homo-erotic relationship and an illicit heterosexual relationship; and such experiences must have enriched incalculably his moral and emotional range as a dramatist.

Accordingly, while some of the plays appear to *condemn* extra-marital copulation, others appear to *condone* it. *A Midsummer Night's Dream* memorably suggests that Bottom enjoys ineffable sexual bliss with Titania; and, if he does, that actually improves the play morally, for we see that the interfering, manipulative Oberon is then hoist with his own petard: his manipulations of others cause him to be cuckolded. Serves him right.

If we turn to *Antony and Cleopatra*, in which Antony marries the virtuous Octavia but is unable to remain faithful to her, Octavia may win our pity, but Antony, entranced by Cleopatra, surely wins our sympathy and may even seem enviable. 'The beds i'th'East are soft'; and Cleopatra proves irresistible. Who, apart from Octavius and Octavia, can blame Antony? Though morality supports Octavia, ontology supports Cleopatra. (Ontology is concerned with essences rather than with moral judgements.) Cleopatra has ontological plenitude; or, as Enobarbus more lucidly puts it:

> Age cannot wither her, nor custom stale
> Her infinite variety: other women cloy
> The appetites they feed, but she makes hungry
> Where most she satisfies...[2]

In this play, more than in any other, Shakespeare lets the claim for ontological fullness, sheer intensity of being, outweigh the claim of morality. Yes, Cleopatra can be mean, cruel, irritating, untruthful, fickle; but she is the fullest female characterisation in the whole of Elizabethan-Jacobean drama; she abounds in sensuous seductive vitality; and only a person with a heart of puritanical stone would condemn Antony for his infidelity to Octavia. In his energies, his eloquence and his demanding sensuality, Antony is the perfect match for Cleopatra; indeed, they 'stand up peerless'.

The claims for intensity of hedonistic experience thus sometimes outweigh the claims of morality in Shakespeare's plays, as they must have done in Shakespeare's life. Although, in *The Tempest*, Prospero enjoins Ferdinand to wait until marriage for fulfilment, this is not an injunction which the young Shakespeare would have respected, to judge from the fact that, just six months after his marriage to Anne Hathaway, his wife gave birth to the couple's first daughter, Susanna. Perhaps Anne would later have sympathised with the pregnant Julietta of *Measure for Measure*.

To conclude. It is true that Shakespeare's plays often make a persuasive case for confining sexual fulfilment to marriage. Sometimes those characters who fulfil their desires extra-maritally are corrupt exemplars of egoistic appetite, and they increase the disorder and violence of their societies. Nevertheless, Shakespeare's combination of realism and romanticism (allied to potent personal experience) also enabled him to depict sympathetically various lovers whose fulfilment lies outside wedlock. Shakespeare was steeped in Christianity, but as a creative artist he often served that god Janus.

Notes:
1. I quote 4.1.19-22 of *The Tempest*, ed. Cedric Watts (Ware: Wordsworth, 2004).
2. *Antony and Cleopatra*, ed. Cedric Watts (Ware: Wordsworth, 2006), 2.2.240-43.

9

A Bum Rap? In *A Midsummer Night's Dream*, Does 'Bottom' Mean 'Bum'? Bottom's Name Anal-ysed.

Who is right about Bottom's name? *The Oxford English Dictionary*? Or readers attuned to vulgarity? You've guessed already. I claim here that Shakespeare backs those profane readers. (If you're not one of them, better not read on; just go forth and multiply. As they say on TV, this item 'contains strong language'.) Let's get stuck in.

Nowadays, one of the connotations of the word 'bottom' is 'buttocks' or, vulgarly for British speakers of English, 'bum'. Consequently, some readers may assume that 'bum' was in Shakespeare's mind when he conferred the name 'Bottom' on the thespian weaver of *A Midsummer Night's Dream* (a play usually dated 1595). Alas, the *Oxford English Dictionary* (*Online*) says No. It declares that 'bottom', in the sense of 'posteriors' or 'sitting part', dates only from the late 18th century. The dictionary cites, as the earliest instance, Erasmus Darwin's *Zoonomia*, 1794-6: 'So as to have his head and shoulders much lower than his bottom'. The problem becomes more complicated when Peter Holland annotates the name 'Bottom' in his 1998 Oxford edition of *A Midsummer Night's Dream*. Holland observes that a 'bottom' was a core on which yarn was wound, and then offers the following intriguing speculation:

> No one has yet proved convincingly that the word 'bottom' could at this date refer to a person's behind; if it could, then the transformation into an ass (arse) would seem almost a literalizing of Bottom's name...[1]

Here, therefore, I ask two questions. First, could 'Bottom' indeed connote 'bum'? Secondly, could it also connote both 'arse' and 'ass'? You can see that if the answer to either question or both questions is

40

'yes', *A Midsummer Night's Dream* becomes an even better play. It becomes thematically richer and wittier.

In the book entitled *Henry V, War Criminal? and Other Shakespeare Puzzles*, I remarked of Bottom: 'His name means "core (or spool) of yarn" (appropriate to a weaver) as well as suggesting "buttocks".' My end-note added:

> It obviously suggests 'buttocks' to modern audiences. Holland... says that there is no proof that 'bottom' had that meaning when Shakespeare was writing. I think it would be unwise to underestimate Shakespeare's associative talents, particularly where the human body is concerned. 'Bottom', at that time, could certainly refer to the base of anything and to the capacious curvature of a ship, so an association with 'buttocks' seems natural enough. [2]

Of course, we have obvious evidence that Shakespeare could associate a comic character with buttocks. In *Measure for Measure* we encounter Pompey Bum, and Escalus (on hearing his name) predictably remarks: 'Troth, and your bum is the greatest thing about you; so that, in the beastliest sense, you are Pompey the Great.' [3] Thus, the surname 'Bum' seems to strengthen the claim that Bottom has a name that could connote 'buttocks'; but, once again, the *Oxford English Dictionary* pronounces its stern veto. The dictionary declares:

> The guess that *bum* is 'a mere contraction of bottom', besides its phonetic difficulties, is at variance with the historical fact that 'bottom' in this sense is found only from the 18th c. [4]

The 'historical fact'? Ask Venus about that. She insolently challenges the dictionary's putative 'historical fact'. In Shakespeare's *Venus and Adonis*, 1593, Venus seductively addresses Adonis thus:

> I'll be a park, and thou shalt be my deer:
> Feed where thou wilt, on mountain or in dale;
>   Graze on my lips, and if those hills be dry,
>   Stray lower, where the pleasant fountains lie.

> Within this limit is relief enough,
> Sweet bottom grass and high delightful plain,
> Round rising hillocks, brakes obscure and rough,
> To shelter thee from tempest and from rain...[5]

Although he lacks the guidance of Eric Partridge's *Shakespeare's Bawdy*, Adonis is bound to interpret 'bottom grass' as 'hair growing in and about the crotch'.[6] And even stronger evidence can be found. In Thomas Dekker's *The Shoemaker's Holiday* (first recorded in 1599, printed in 1600), Sybil tells Rose this:

> My Lord Mayor your father, and Master Philpot your uncle, and Master Scott your cousin, and Mistress Frigbottom, by Doctors' Commons, do all, by my troth, send you most hearty commendations.[7]

'Frigbottom'? What does the *Oxford English Dictionary* say this time? At last, it helpfully plumbs the depths. It cites John Florio's 'frig', 1598 (*'Fricciare*, to frig, to wriggle, to tickle'), under the heading '**frig**, *v*[*erb*] ...3. Freq. used with euphemistic force. **a.** *trans.* and *intr.* = FUCK *v.* 1. **b.** To masturbate.' Thus, the surname of Mistress Frigbottom is equivalent at least to 'Wrigglebottom' or 'Tickle-Bum', possibly to some grosser name such as 'Wank-Fanny', and probably to some name invoking sexual intercourse such as 'Shag-Arse'. The reference to 'Doctors' Commons' suggests that her clients would be young lawyers. ('Commons' here may mean not only 'college' but also 'brothels': *Measure for Measure* refers to 'abuses in common houses'.)

Hence, there is good evidence that, in Shakespeare's day, 'bottom' could indeed mean 'posteriors' or 'bum'. It indicates that *O.E.D.*'s date for that meaning, 1794-6, may be two centuries too late; and it enriches *A Midsummer Night's Dream*. In that comedy, Shakespeare exploits various connotations of 'bottom', and we now find that they include not only 'core or spool of yarn or thread', 'foundation in reality', 'substance' and 'limit', but also 'bum'. We may recall Robin

Goodfellow's gleeful words, in Act II, scene i, about the aunt who mistakes his crouching form for a foot-stool:

> Then slip I from her bum, down topples she,
> And 'Tailor!' cries, and falls into a cough...

(Probably 'Tailor' here means 'My tail': i.e. 'My prat', as in the modern 'pratfall'.) [8] Furthermore, by joining 'bottom' with 'nether regions of the body, perhaps the arse', Mistress Frigbottom goes halfway to verifying Holland's speculation that the metamorphosis of Bottom into ass is a literalizing of the weaver's name.

One obvious difficulty remains. In Shakespeare's works generally, 'ass' refers either to the quadruped, the beast of burden, or, metaphorically, to a foolish person. Eric Partridge claims that sometimes 'ass' implies 'arse', but his examples seem generally unconvincing: for instance, 'May not an ass know when the cart draws the horse?' in *King Lear*.[9] Here 'arse' doesn't fit, but 'fool' and 'the quadruped' do. Current American usage, in which the spelling and sound of 'ass' denote the human backside far more frequently than they denote the beast of burden, may mislead some readers of *A Midsummer Night's Dream*.[10] In Shakespeare's era, various plays, notably John Lyly's *Midas* and *Endimion*, indicate an aural distinction between 'ass' and 'arse', the former noun having a short 'a'.

Nevertheless, in English west-country parlance, 'ass', like the liturgical 'mass', has often been pronounced with a long or intermediate 'a', as in rural Gloucestershire's 'You silly aass!'. So I think it would be rash to rule out the occasional occurrence of that pronunciation amid the evolving diversity of Elizabethan English with its regional and social variations. An ambiguous shift into rhyme in the anonymous *The Taming of a Shrew* may perhaps offer an instance of the long 'a', and is certainly further evidence of the swift associability of 'ass' with 'arse':

> *Val*[*eria*] Well, will you plaie a little?
> *Kate* I, give me the Lute.
> *She plaies*
> *Val.* That stop was false, play it againe.

> *Kate* Then mend it thou, thou filthy asse.
> *Val.* What, doo you bid me kisse your arse?
> *Kate* How now jack sause, your a jollie mate,
> Your best be still least I crosse your pate,
> And make your musicke flie about your eares.
> Ile make it and your foolish coxcombe meet.[11]

The question here, obviously, is: 'Where does the rhyming pattern begin?'. If the words 'Then mend it' begin a rhyming couplet, then here 'asse' (i.e. 'ass') may sound much like 'arse'; but if the start of the pattern is 'How now', it probably does not. In this passage, choosing between two couplets and one is difficult.

Shakespeare relished significant names. For example, when Romeo first meets Juliet, he is disguised as a pilgrim, a guise true to his name: because *romeo* is Italian for 'pilgrim to Rome'. Juliet, true to her name, was born in July. In a later play, Iago's name, ominously for Othello the Moor, is not Italian (as we would expect in a drama depicting Venetians) but Spanish, so that it evokes Spain's patron saint: Santiago Matamoros: Saint James the Moor-Slayer. Iago's follower Roderigo, who hopes to cuckold Othello, bears virtually the same Christian name as Rodrigo Díaz de Bivar, 'El Cid', the legendary enemy of Moors.

I think, therefore, that the possibility should remain that Bottom's asinine disguise, too, has onomastical aptness. His surname, which certainly connotes 'bum', and almost certainly connotes 'arse', can sometimes evoke and may occasionally connote 'ass'. When Quince says to the metamorphosed weaver, 'Bless thee, Bottom, bless thee! Thou art translated',[12] he possibly means by the latter clause not only 'You are changed' but also 'Your name, "Bottom", has been translated – converted from air into flesh – via "arse" into "ass".' And we recall that a name which also suggests 'lowness, base' has been conferred on a character who, with Titania, has attained the height of bliss.

Thus Shakespeare, ever resourceful, ever keen to solidify the abstract (as his similes and metaphors attest), gratifies present-day appetites for both the subtly semiotic and the carnally vulgar. In a way, the name symbolises some of the paradoxical strengths of Shakespearian drama, in which buffoonery and the carnivalesque provide the counterpoint to subtlety and (sometimes tragic) complexity.

Notes:
1. William Shakespeare: *A Midsummer Night's Dream*, ed. Peter Holland (Oxford: Oxford University Press, 1998), p. 147 n.
2. John Sutherland and Cedric Watts: *Henry V, War Criminal? and Other Shakespeare Puzzles* (Oxford: Oxford University Press, 2000), pp. 213-14. *O.E.D.* gives 1522 as its earliest date for the nautical "bottom", "the part of the hull of the ship which is below the wales". Ann Thompson's edition of *The Taming of the Shrew* (Cambridge: Cambridge University Press, 1985), p. 130, annotates Grumio's "beat me to death with a bottom of brown thread" thus: "**bottom**: spool, bobbin. (With obscene reference as well.)"
3. William Shakespeare: *Measure for Measure*, ed. Cedric Watts (Ware: Wordsworth, 2005), 2.1.201-3.
4. *Op. cit.*, entry for "bum".
5. Lines 231-8. William Shakespeare: *The Poems*, ed. F. T. Prince (London: Methuen, 1969), pp. 15-16.
6. Eric Partridge: *Shakespeare's Bawdy* (London: Routledge, 1968), pp. 69-70.
7. Thomas Dekker: *The Shoemaker's Apprentice*, ed. R. L. Smallwood and Stanley Wells (Manchester: Manchester University Press, 1979), sc. 2, lines 22-5 (pp. 98-9). 'Bottom' meaning both 'boat' and 'vagina' is found in Sir John Davies's *The Scourge of Folly* (London: Richard Redmer, 1611), p. 155: 'Phryne will haue an Oare in each mans Boate, / While she sinks theirs that in her Bottom floate.'
8. Cf. 'Prick the woman's tailor': 3.2.158-9 of *The Second Part of King Henry IV*, ed. A. R. Humphreys (London: Methuen, 1966), and Humphreys' notes to lines 149 and 151, all on p. 104. In *The Tempest*, Act 2, sc. 2, Stephano sings of a Kate who disliked sailors, but 'A tailor might scratch her where'er she did itch'.'Tail' (meaning 'nether region of the body') could refer to the anus, vulva, or penis.

9. Partridge, p. 59. Occasionally, Partridge (though an admirable pioneer in the area) seems over-zealous in his quest for the bawdy.

10. In recent years, the common American usage has increasingly infiltrated the British lexicon. For instance, in *The Times*, 19.2.2009, p. 77, the cricketer Mike Atherton wrote: 'It is Stanford's ass now giving a great, whopping moonie'. (The American 'ass' is sometimes merely a derogatory synecdoche for 'self', as in 'Get your ass over here!'.)

11. *The Taming of a Shrew* in *Narrative and Dramatic Sources of Shakespeare*, Vol. 1, ed. Geoffrey Bullough (London: Routledge & Kegan Paul, 1957), p. 82.

12. See 3.1.108 of *A Midsummer Night's Dream*, ed. Cedric Watts (Ware: Wordsworth, 2002).

10

Who is the 'Manager of Mirth'?
In *A Midsummer Night's Dream*, Act 5, is it Philostrate or Egeus?

In the Arden text of *A Midsummer Night's Dream* edited by Harold Brooks, you will find that during Act 5, scene 1, there is a sequence of dialogue about possible entertainments for the marriage festivities.

The options include 'The battle with the Centaurs, to be sung / By an Athenian eunuch to the harp', 'The riot of the tipsy Bacchanals, / Tearing the Thracian singer in their rage', 'The thrice three Muses mourning for the death / Of learning', and, of course, the 'very tragical mirth' of the Pyramus and Thisbe (or Thisby) play. Theseus discusses them, appropriately enough, with Philostrate, his 'usual manager of mirth'. But, if you turn to the Oxford text of *A Midsummer Night's Dream* edited by Peter Holland, you will find that Philostrate has vanished from this scene. Now his words are spoken by, of all people, the crusty Egeus, while the titles of the proposed performances are read out not by Theseus, as was the case formerly, but by Lysander.[1]

What is the explanation of these remarkable changes? And who is right?

Harold Brooks followed the First Quarto text (Q1, 1600) of *A Midsummer Night's Dream*, while Peter Holland followed the First Folio (F1, 1623). Why does F1 differ so much in these places? A materialistic explanation could be this: that at some point after the Q1 version had been performed, the acting company saw a way to save money. They made changes in order to eliminate the actor needed for Philostrate (who previously had made only a brief appearance, in Act 1). Another editor, R. A. Foakes, suggests that Philostrate, though present in Act 1, might have been eliminated as a speaking-part at least, thus effecting an economy.[2] Peter Holland, however, claims (p. 266) that there is no 'doubling scheme' which would 'enable the company to economize on speaking actors by substituting Egeus for Philostrate in Act 5'.

In any case, the change made in F1 introduced glaring inconsistencies. Egeus, the crusty, intolerant father of Hermia, is a wildly unlikely sudden choice as Master of the Revels. That would be like hiring a resentful undertaker to arrange a festive celebration. Egeus is certainly not the 'usual manager of mirth', for in Act 1, it was definitely Philostrate who was ordered by Theseus to arrange 'merriments'. Furthermore, perhaps as a result of misreading by a hasty compositor, one of the speeches in the Act 5 sequence of F1 is still attributed to Philostrate instead of being re-allocated.

Peter Holland argues that the re-distribution of words to Egeus and Lysander in this sequence enriches the characterisation and themes of the play. In Q1, Egeus is absent from Act 5: no stage-direction indicates his presence. But if he is absent, then the question of his attitude to the resolution of conflict remains unresolved. In F1, he is conspicuously present. As Holland says, 'F's text allows Egeus' incorporation in the Athenian society at the end of the play to be visible'. His attitude to his daughter and her husband may be hostile or acquiescent – that will depend on the particular production of the play. But whatever that attitude is, the production can make it evident to the audience, so that the plot-sequence concerning Egeus's hostility to the lovers can here reach a termination.

Furthermore (this argument goes), that version of the last scene generates a thematic irony. In Act 4, scene 1, Egeus demanded punishment for the disobedient lovers, Hermia and Lysander. He was over-ruled by Theseus. In Act 5, Egeus tries to persuade Theseus not to approve the performance of the 'Pyramus and Thisbe' play. Again, he is over-ruled by Theseus. On the first occasion, a marriage opposed by Egeus is permitted. On the second occasion, Theseus allows a performance of a drama which, though comic, displays a tragedy in which love is destroyed by death: a commentary on Egeus's demand that the disobedient lovers receive a death-sentence. The double over-ruling averts *real* death and permits *feigned* death.

Well, that is an ingenious defence of the F1 version; but you may think that it founders on the following objections. First, as was mentioned, it is fully appropriate that Philostrate, the appointed Master of the Revels, should re-appear when revels are being discussed and selected. In contrast, it is obviously inappropriate that a harsh father should appear unexpectedly to undertake this job. Given that Egeus was over-ruled by Theseus in the crucial matter of the marriage of the disobedient daughter, it is entirely understandable that Egeus should be absent (presumably smouldering bitterly in anger, disappointment and resentment) from the joviality of Act 5.

But would the absence of an important character from the stage at the play's close be Shakespearian? Actually, the answer is Yes. The famous example is the Fool in *King Lear*. What happens to him? In some productions, Lear's 'And my poor fool is hanged' is staged in such a way as to suggest that the Fool has been killed by Albany's forces or has perhaps committed suicide. Editors, however, usually interpret 'poor fool' as Lear's term of endearment for Cordelia, in which case the jester remains unaccounted for. (One explanation is that the actor doubled the rôle of Cordelia, so her presence entails the Fool's absence.) If the loyal Fool can be strangely absent from the dénouement of that great tragedy, there seems no reason to object to the quite credible absence of the truculent Egeus from the dénouement of *A Midsummer Night's Dream*. That would suit his joyless and inflexible character. (But I'll return to that matter of Lear's Fool later in this book.) We may also recall the treatment of the censorious but unfortunate Malvolio at the dénouement of *Twelfth Night*: while others are reconciled, Malvolio, threatening revenge, bitterly departs.

In short, the F1 text of *A Midsummer Night's Dream* may represent playhouse practice, but Q1 seems closer to what Shakespeare originally wrote and intended. So, when the editorial opportunity came my way, I gladly restored mirth-manager Philostrate to the play's Act 5.[3] Wouldn't you?

Notes:
1. *A Midsummer Night's Dream*, ed. Harold F. Brooks (London: Methuen, 1979). *A Midsummer Night's Dream*, ed. Peter Holland (Oxford: Oxford University Press, 1994; rpt., 1998).
2. *A Midsummer Night's Dream*, ed. R. A. Foakes (Cambridge: Cambridge University Press, 1984), p. 141.
3. *A Midsummer Night's Dream*, ed. Cedric Watts (Ware: Wordsworth, 2002).

11

A Vanishing Trick in *A Midsummer Night's Dream*: Where is the Wedding Song? And Why is Recycling Apt?

In the closing minutes of *A Midsummer Night's Dream*, Oberon instructs the fairies to sing a song after him and to dance it 'trippingly'. Titania then says that the fairy singers will 'bless this place'. Next, Oberon, in the speech beginning 'Now, until the break of day', predicts and pronounces an elaborate blessing on the place, its newlyweds and its owner. The puzzle is: where are the words of the song that Oberon introduces – or of the songs, if Titania's promise is the cue for another? The early texts do not supply them.

Dr Johnson, long ago, thought that two songs were implied, even though their words were not provided: one introduced by Oberon and another introduced by Titania. In the First Folio's text of the play (F1), however, the speech by Oberon which begins 'Now, until the break of day' is preceded by the heading *'The Song'*. Some editors, therefore, assume that this solves the problem and that his words after the heading, from 'Now' until he leaves the stage, are really the lyric.

The trouble with this notion is that Oberon's speech does not resemble the normal Shakespearian lyric. It lacks a distinctive stanza-form and refrain. It sounds directive rather than lyrical.

> Now, until the break of day,
> Through the house each fairy stray
> To the best bride-bed will we,
> Which by us shall blessèd be:
> And the issue there create
> Ever shall be fortunate...

Even that word 'Now', in his 'Now, until the break of day', suggests a fresh start *after* a song. Quite likely, F1's heading results from a compositor's misreading of a prompt-book's reference to a song which is now absent. But, if a director of the play adopts the reasonable view that Oberon and Titania introduce one lyric, what can that person do to fill the gap? Where can we find an appropriate song?

In 1912, Harley Granville Barker brilliantly filled the gap by deploying there the song which, at the beginning of the later play *The Two Noble Kinsmen*, graces a wedding – the nuptials of (by lucky coincidence) Theseus and Hippolyta! Thus the opening of one play featuring this couple completes the close of another play featuring them. As for its aptness, even to the blessing of the 'bride-house', that speaks for itself:

> Roses, their sharp spines being gone,
> Not royal in their smells alone
>   But in their hue;
> Maiden pinks, of odour faint,
> Daisies smell-less, yet most quaint,
>   And sweet thyme true;
>
> Primrose, firstborn child of Ver,
> Merry Springtime's harbinger,
>   With harebells dim;
> Oxlips, in their cradles growing,
> Marigolds on deathbeds blowing,
>   Lark's-heels trim:
>
> All dear Nature's children sweet
> Lie 'fore bride and bridegroom's feet
>   Blessing their sense.
> Not an angel of the air,
> Bird melodious or bird fair,
>   Is absent hence.
>
> The crow, the slanderous cuckoo, nor
> The boding raven, nor chough hoar,
>   Nor chattering pie,
> May on our bride-house perch or sing,

Or with them any discord bring,
   But from it fly.[1]

It's a fine nuptial lyric, completely appropriate to the situation and mood of the ending of *A Midsummer Night's Dream*. Its natural imagery is fully Shakespearian, echoing a range of passages elsewhere. A 'crimson rose' was cited earlier in the play. *Romeo and Juliet* punningly exploits the name 'pink'. Daisies arise in *Love's Labour's Lost* and *Hamlet*. Thyme grew earlier in the *Dream* and is cited in *Othello*. The primrose, oxlip and marigold appear in Perdita's floral catalogue in *The Winter's Tale*, and the primrose is linked to the harebell in *Cymbeline*. The oxlip was also mentioned previously in the *Dream*. Crows and ravens are birds of ill-omen, notably in *Julius Cæsar*. That 'slanderous cuckoo', slanderous because he reminds men that husbands may be cuckolded, features in numerous plays (notably the ending of *Love's Labour's Lost*), including – already – the *Dream*. Choughs are gabbling birds, according to *All's Well*, while *Macbeth* states that choughs and magpies have helped to reveal sinister secrets. Thus, the song's imagery harmonizes with Shakespeare's customary usages.

A sceptic might, of course, say: 'Wait a minute. You're taking a song from *The Two Noble Kinsmen*? Isn't that an apocryphal work?' Well, there's a growing scholarly consensus that that play was written jointly by William Shakespeare and John Fletcher. More to the point, there is also a strong consensus that of the two authors, Shakespeare wrote Act 1, scene 1, which contains the song.[2] It seems to me a reasonable hypothesis that this lyric was first written by Shakespeare for *A Midsummer Night's Dream* and that later he used it again in *The Two Noble Kinsmen*. We know that the playwright did repeat a lyric elsewhere: *Twelfth Night* ends with a Clown's song (which has the refrain 'hey, ho, the wind and the rain:…the rain it raineth every day'), and years later, in *King Lear*, a verse with the same refrain is sung by the Fool.

To re-use a song would, in principle, have Shakespeare's full approval, for the playwright was a master of recycling. Perhaps he was inspired by the vernal renewal in the progress of the seasons. Or perhaps he learned from Titus Andronicus, who thoughtfully recycles Demetrius and Chiron in a pie to be eaten by their mother, Tamora. Shakespeare ransacked countless books for material to be re-used in his plays. He exploited Holinshed in *Richard II* and *Henry IV*, and Plutarch in *Julius Cæsar* and *Antony and Cleopatra*. He recycled characters from one play in another: Octavius, Antony, Hal, Henry IV and Falstaff come immediately to mind. The type of the fallible martial hero reappears: Titus Andronicus, Hotspur, Othello, Antony, Coriolanus (and perhaps even Armado, if I'm right about *Love's Labours Won*). Situations are recycled, as when lovers part sadly at dawn not only in *Romeo and Juliet* but also in *Troilus and Cressida*; and the later aubade accentuates the bitter-sweetness. A family is sundered during a storm: in the early *Comedy of Errors* as well as the late romances, *The Winter's Tale* and *The Tempest*. Indeed, when you consider the central themes of *The Winter's Tale* and *The Tempest* (regeneration after destruction, new life after apparent death), you'll see that recycling *itself* is recycled.

Furthermore, Shakespeare's jokes about cuckolds and their horns are so frequent that his audiences must have found them repeatedly funny. Those gags, however, have eventually become 'alms for oblivion', eminently forgettable. In such cases, Ben Jonson for once was wrong: because, when repeating such jests, Shakespeare was evidently *not* writing 'for all time'.

Notes:
1. I quote the text as given in *A Midsummer Night's Dream*, ed. Cedric Watts (Ware: Wordsworth 2004), pp. 109-10.
2. See, for example, the evidence surveyed in Brian Vickers' *Shakespeare, Co-Author* (Oxford: Oxford University Press, 2002).

12

The Mysterious Mobility of Salarino (or is He Really Salerio?).

In *The Merchant of Venice*, there's a tricky puzzle concerning Salarino. He seems to be in two places at once. How can this be? Has Shakespeare blundered?

In Act 2, scene 6, Salarino apparently goes along to the masque with Jessica and Lorenzo. In Act 2, scene 8, he reports the poignant parting of Bassanio from Antonio at the quayside. So what's the problem? It's obvious. That parting coincided with the time of the masque. If Salarino was attending that masque, he could not also have been a quayside observer of Bassanio and Antonio. What complicates matters is that, as so often in Shakespeare, the original stage-directions are more sparse or casual than we would wish them to be.

At 2.6.58-9 (in my edition), the eloping Jessica, disguised as a boy, enters to meet her masquing lover Lorenzo, whose companions, Salarino and Gratiano, are also dressed as masquers. Lorenzo there says:

> What, art thou come? On, gentlemen, away;
> Our masquing mates by this time for us stay.[1]

The play's First Quarto (Q1) and First Folio (F1) then give the stage-direction '*Exit*', but arguably it should be '*Exeunt*', for Lorenzo then departs with Jessica and, it would seem, with the 'Sally' who is present, namely Salarino (if spelt a little erratically), according to those early texts. Gratiano, starting to follow them, is suddenly detained by Antonio, who, arriving in haste, urges him to go to the ship which 'Bassanio presently will go aboard'. So how, in view of this, can Salarino report Bassanio's farewell?

55

Professor M. M. Mahood once proposed an ingenious solution to this problem. (It's on p. 110 of her 2003 Cambridge edition of the play.) She envisaged that, instead of accompanying Jessica and Lorenzo offstage, Salarino remains alongside Gratiano to be addressed by Antonio. But what, then, of Lorenzo's words 'On, gentlemen, away', which appear to be ushering offstage Salarino as well as Gratiano? The plural, 'gentlemen', must obviously denote both of them. Mahood, however, notes that though F1 has the plural, Q1 has the singular, 'gentleman'; and thus, since Jessica is wearing masculine attire, 'gentleman' could be a jocular way of referring to her alone.

This is ingenious; but several objections come to mind. The first is that Jessica is disguised as a page-boy, not a gentleman. Secondly, 'gentlemen' seems to be a naturally appropriate plural, since Lorenzo is fully aware of the presence of two male friends, Salarino and Gratiano, who, being dressed as masquers themselves, obviously intend to accompany him to the masque. More objections arise when Antonio, having entered and detained Gratiano, says 'Where are all the rest?' (evidently meaning 'By yourself? Where have all the others gone?'). The dialogue between Antonio and Gratiano gives a consistent impression that nobody else is present. It continues with Antonio saying:

> 'Tis nine o'clock: our friends all stay for you.
> No masque tonight: the wind is come about;
> Bassanio presently will go aboard.
> I have sent twenty out to seek for you.

Gratiano then responds: 'I am glad on't. I desire no more delight'. He does not say: 'We are glad on't. We desire no more delight', as he probably would if Salarino were present. And in that case, you would expect Salarino to add a corroborating response; but there is none.

It seems, therefore, much more appropriate to assume that Salarino made his exit with Jessica and Bassanio. But that leads us back to the original problem. How can Salarino, if he is attending a masque, be also present at the quayside?

There is an elegant way of rescuing consistency. We need only assume that when Antonio says 'No masque tonight', he does not mean 'No masque for *you*, my friend, tonight'. Instead, we interpret his meaning as: 'No masque for *anyone* tonight, because (apart from Jessica and Lorenzo, the runaways) all the people who would have attended it, our friends and associates, are being re-directed to the harbour for the farewells there, as the wind has changed favourably, and no time must be lost before the ship sails.' Thus, although Salarino has headed for the masque with Jessica and Lorenzo, he will soon find himself being re-directed to the quayside. (As for Jessica and Lorenzo: the masque being cancelled, they proceed overland to Genoa, before coincidentally meeting another 'Sally', Salerio, and proceeding with him to Belmont.) At the quayside, Salarino will witness the departure of Bassanio and Gratiano under sail, so that he can then report the event to the third 'Sally', actually a 'Solly', Solanio. Thus, consistency is restored.

If my reasoning doesn't convince you, don't worry. You get two consolations. The first is that the inconsistency you are left with is peripheral to the main dramatic interest: it may not seem important. The second consolation is that it leads you to consideration of the numerous apparent inconsistencies in Shakespeare; consideration which often ends in an enhanced sense of his genius. Indeed, it is tempting to venture the following rule for Shakespeare's plays: the greater the work, the more glaring are its inconsistencies. Certainly, *Hamlet*, *Othello* and *King Lear* illustrate the rule.

Of course, by now you will have spotted the 'Three Sallies' puzzle. Some editors of *The Merchant of Venice* preserve all three Sallies: Salarino, Salerio and Solanio. Other editors, among them John Dover Wilson, reduce the three to two, believing that Shakespeare is unlikely to have induced confusion by using three similar names, and that 'Salarino' is merely a variant of 'Salerio'. Nevertheless, I prefer to respect Q1 and F1 in preserving all three. In any case, Salerio is distinctively introduced in Act 3, scene 2, as '*a messenger from Venice*', which would be unnecessary if he were one of the Sallies we had met previously. If you doubt that Shakespeare would use three similar names, remember that in *Julius Cæsar* we find not only two characters called 'Cinna' but also two called 'Flavius', while in *As You Like It* two characters bear the name 'Jaques' and the name 'Oliver' is borne by another two.

These interlinked puzzles about Salarino neatly prove that Shakespeare's works combine the elegance of high art with the untidiness of everyday reality. Indeed, it's that untidiness which largely generates Shakespeare's historical immortality. Why? Because it makes everyone (readers, critics, editors, actors and directors, at least) repeatedly *try to tidy him up*. Shakespeare is the master of the seductive muddle.

Note:
1. *The Merchant of Venice*, ed. Cedric Watts (Ware: Wordsworth, 2000).

13

The Puzzle of the Two Hals in *Henry IV, Part 2.*

In *Henry IV, Part 2*, numerous characters express the view that when Hal, Prince Henry, comes to power on the death of his father, King Henry IV, disorder and misrule will prevail.

When Falstaff hears of that death, he immediately assumes that his time of dominance has arrived, and justice will be overthrown. As he puts it:

> Let us take any man's horses: the laws of England are at my commandment. Blessed are they that have been my friends, and woe to my Lord Chief Justice!

The ailing Henry IV had anticipated that anarchy would ensue when Hal succeeded him. Here is his dismal view of what Hal will do:

> Give that which gave thee life unto the worms;
> Pluck down my officers; break my decrees;
> For now a time is come to mock at form:
> Harry the Fifth is crowned! Up, vanity!
> Down, royal state! All you sage counsellors, hence!
> And to the English court assemble now,
> From every region, apes of idleness!...
> For the fifth Harry from curbed licence plucks
> The muzzle of restraint...

Furthermore, when Hal is crowned King, the Lord Chief Justice immediately becomes a figure of anxiety and trepidation. This is because, in the past, when he was presiding in the court of law, Hal had boxed his ear, and he had promptly sentenced the Prince to jail. Now that eminent representative of law and order fears harsh retribution.

What is so puzzling about all this is that Falstaff, Henry IV and the Lord Chief Justice are talking of a Hal quite different from the Hal we have seen, the heir to the throne that Shakespeare has depicted in detail in both parts of *Henry IV*. Early in *Henry IV, Part 1*, Hal, in his first soliloquy (at the end of Act 1, scene 2), had made quite clear to us that though he was accompanying rogues, he was maintaining a critical distance from them:

> I know you all, and will a while uphold
> The unyoked humour of your idleness.
> Yet herein will I imitate the sun,
> Who doth permit the base contagious clouds
> To smother up his beauty from the world,
> That when he please again to be himself,
> Being wanted, he may be more wondered at,
> By breaking through the foul and ugly mists
> Of vapour that did seem to strangle him.

While associating with (and certainly having some fun with) Falstaff and his associates, the Prince is never actually defiled by their pitch. At the Gad's Hill robbery, Hal does not rob the King's Exchequer: on the contrary, he robs the robbers, and later we learn that he has repaid to the authorities (with interest) the briefly-stolen loot. We never see him breaking the law. At no point does Shakespeare depict that notorious incident in which Hal boxes the ear of the Lord Chief Justice. Nor is it feasible that the Hal we see in these two plays would ever do such a thing. He had even (in *1 Henry IV*, Act 2, sc. 4) given Falstaff emphatic early warning that he would eventually banish the fat knight.

In short, *Henry IV, Part 2* offers us two contradictory Hals. One, shown in detail, is the basically law-abiding Hal who merely enjoys raffish company and plans to spring a pleasant surprise by revealing eventually that he is not the rogue he is thought to be. The other, understood, recalled and reported by Falstaff, Henry IV and the Lord Chief Justice, is a truly law-breaking, dangerously anarchic figure. That latter figure, the rogue who boxed the Justice's ear, was indeed well known to Elizabethan theatre-goers, but not from Shakespeare's plays. They knew him from the popular anonymous play, *The Famous Victories of Henry V*, which enacted before the theatre-goers' eyes the rowdy scene of Hal abusing and hitting Justice. There Hal was seeking to rescue an associate who, having committed a robbery at Gad's Hill, had been sentenced to death. Officers, obeying the Justice, consequently carried Hal away to jail.

The Hal of *Henry IV, Part 2* is, then, a contradictory figure. He is partly Shakespeare's Hal, a basically law-abiding heir to the throne, an astute ruler in the making; and he is partly (as recalled by various characters) the riotous law-breaking Hal of *The Famous Victories*. For the purposes of dramatic interest, Shakespeare has made his Hal a recurrent character of a most peculiar kind. In *Part 2*, the Prince has obvious continuity with the calculating, good Hal of *Henry IV, Part 1*; but he also has continuity with the bad Hal of *The Famous Victories*. Of course, both Shakespeare's Hal and the Hal of *Famous Victories* emerge as morally sound and heroic kings. In the latter case, though, there is a real, very late conversion from the lawless Hal to the law-abiding Henry V. In the former case, no conversion is needed, for the observable Hal of the *Henry IV* plays was always law-abiding. We see that in *2 Henry IV*, he scorns Poins ('What a disgrace is it to me to remember thy name!'), insults Falstaff ('You whoreson candle-mine you'), says that Doll Tearsheet 'should be some road' (meaning 'some whore'), and, in contrast to his namesake in *The Famous Victories*, who impatiently desired his father's death, is melancholy when his father is ill – yet that king (whose elder son, Hal, had once rescued him on a battlefield) alleges that Hal impatiently desires his father's death.

The sound Hal that we generally observe is Shakespeare's; the unsound Hal that characters describe and recall is apparently someone else's – a legendary hell-raiser. (Even the sound Hal invokes him by saying, falsely, after his coronation, 'The tide of blood in me / Hath proudly flowed in vanity till now.') This is markedly different from what normally happens when one character spans two or more literary works. The context changes, but usually the character remains consistent: 'transtextual characterisation'. For example, Joseph Conrad's Tom Lingard is the same character in the three novels in which he appears. In bizarre contrast, what Shakespeare apparently offers is the amalgamation in *Henry IV Part 2* of two quite different characters, Shakespeare's Prince Henry and someone else's: a pair of quarrelsome Siamese twins linked by the ligament of a common name: Henry, the Prince of Wales.

The solution to this puzzle of the seemingly contradictory characterisation of Hal is – I submit – provided by *Richard II*. In that play, when Bullingbrooke (also known as Bolingbroke) gains power, becoming Henry IV, he expresses anxiety about Hal:

> Can no man tell me of my unthrifty son?...
> If any plague hangs over us, 'tis he...
> Inquire at London, 'mongst the taverns there...

Henry IV states that Hal consorts with, and supports, 'unrestrainèd loose companions' who include robbers; and Harry Percy reports the Prince's insolent disobedience, confirming that the brothel-visiting Prince is, in his father's words, 'As dissolute as desperate'. The King nevertheless discerns 'some sparks of better hope', sparks indicating that Hal may reform.

We can, therefore, postulate that the Hal who struck the Lord Chief Justice is the Hal of *Richard II*, who is there said to support the robbers; and that, between Act 5, scene 3, of *Richard II*, and the revealing soliloquy which concludes Act 1, scene 2, of *1 Henry IV*, Hal has matured and has changed from a law-breaking to a law-abiding Prince.

Of course, we are here using conjecture to restore consistency and plausibility by filling a gap in the characterisation: we are making explicit what Shakespeare declines to do. It was *ever* thus. Shakespeare's plays (like his Sonnets) are characterised by the combination of (a) a rich plenitude of information and (b) tantalising reticences, silences or lacunae. That's the combination which nourishes the interpretative industry around Shakespeare; an industry that includes countless stage performances.

We may, therefore, elicit the following axiom of Shakespearian interpretation. *The hole is an essential part of the perennial whole; it is the 'nothing' about which there will always be 'much ado'.*

Note:
I quote *Richard II*, ed. Cedric Watts (Ware: Wordsworth, 2013) and 'Henry *IV, Part One*' and '*Henry IV, Part Two*, ed. Cedric Watts (Ware: Wordsworth, 2013).

14

Should We Save Innogen in *Much Ado about Nothing*?

For centuries, editors have answered that question with a ruthless 'No'. I say 'Yes', and argue here that she should be restored to the play to which she belongs. The main puzzle is: why was she ever suppressed? This is not a trivial matter. You'll soon see that it has big implications for editors, directors and theatre-goers.

Everyone knows about the character called 'Imogen', who has an important rôle in *Cymbeline*, and whose name should be 'Innogen', according (for example) to Roger Warren.[1] Although 'Innogen' probably derived from the Gaelic 'Inghean', meaning 'maiden' or 'daughter', to modern readers it looks like a portmanteau-word suggesting 'innocent from birth'. Apparently the name was misprinted in *Cymbeline*, perhaps because the written version was unclear; and from that play 'Imogen' has been transmitted to posterity, so that it is now a familiar first name for females: Imogen Thomas, the television personality, Imogen Ryall, the Brighton jazz singer, and Imogen Stubbs, the star of stage and screen, come to mind.

Hardly anyone, however, has heard of Innogen in *Much Ado about Nothing*. She is the wife of Leonato and mother of Hero, and she's supposed to appear in at least two scenes. Nevertheless, for centuries, editors (and they always seem to be male editors) have excised her: they've killed the unfortunate woman! You won't find her in such standard editions of the *Complete Works* as Peter Alexander's, or the Riverside, or the Norton, or the Wells and Taylor volume for Oxford. A. R. Humphreys' Arden edition of the play excludes her, and so do the editions by David Stevenson (Signet), Sheldon P. Zitner (Oxford), and John F. Cox (Cambridge). And the list could be extended for many lines. It looks like the perfect crime: no body can be found.

64

What makes this habitual exclusion so strange is that Innogen is clearly specified in the earliest texts from which all subsequent texts derive. They are the First Quarto and the First Folio. In the First Quarto (Q1), the stage-direction for the opening of the play says: '*Enter Leonato gouernour of Messina, Innogen his wife, Hero his daughter, and Beatrice his neece, with a messenger.*' In the First Folio (F1) the stage-direction is almost identical, again specifying '*Innogen his wife*'. At the opening of Act 2, in F1, and at the equivalent location in Q1, the entry of Innogen is yet again specified: '*Leonato, his brother, his wife...*'.

So why do editors delete her? One reason is that she does not say anything. Various editors therefore believe that although Shakespeare introduced her with the intention of giving her a speaking rôle, he found no use for her. Therefore, these editors presume, they are helping Shakespeare by doing what *he* should have done: they are tidying the text (and perhaps reducing the wage-bill) by removing a redundant character. They think they know better than Heminge and Condell, Shakespeare's colleagues, who prepared the First Folio, who must have seen how the play worked in the theatre, and who *retained* Innogen.

What the censorious male editors fail to see is a glaring irony. *Much Ado about Nothing* is a bitter-sweet comedy which strikingly displays the operations of male chauvinism. It shows that women may be treated as adjuncts to the men, to be variously used, abused, manipulated, slandered, discredited or marginalised. By their ruthless dispatch of Innogen, these male editors emulate the cruelty of Claudio. He, totally misled, denounces his fiancée at the altar, so that she, instead of joining him in holy wedlock, is proclaimed a whore, swoons away, and is left by him for dead. When Claudio realises his error, he is (to make amends) quite willing to accept from Leonato a bride – supposedly Leonato's niece – whom, he believes, he has never met! Meanwhile, Beatrice, who has displayed plenty of independent spirit in her bouts of wit with Benedick, eventually agrees to marry her sparring-partner; but will her independence survive years of marriage and, presumably, motherhood?

Part of the answer is provided by the silence of Innogen. In an ironic master-stroke, Shakespeare has, from the very start of the play, established that in this male-dominated world, a wife and mother may be a mute witness of events; a person ignored, not consulted; a person whose later absence from the action expresses eloquently the ways in which some women may be utterly marginalised. She, bearing that name redolent of innocence, is an appropriately passive mother to the much-manipulated and much-demeaned Hero.

In Act 1, scene 1, when Don Pedro says to Leonato, about Hero, 'I think this is your daughter', Leonato replies: 'Her mother hath many times told me so.'[2] This proves that Shakespeare regards this mother as a continuing living presence, for Leonato says 'hath...told', not 'told'. What's more, if she is on stage, as the directions specify, we may imagine her expression (perhaps good-humoured, or resigned, or disgusted) as she hears that ironic exchange of dialogue and its bawdy continuation. The continuation jocularly implies that if Benedick had been older, he might well have copulated with Innogen, thus casting subsequent doubt on Hero's legitimacy. 'Were you in doubt, sir, that you asked her?', enquires Benedick; and Leonato coarsely responds: 'Signor Benedick, no, for then you were a child.' Grossly embarrassing material for the listening mother.

By erasing Innogen from *Much Ado about Nothing*, the male editors of the work have both *weakened* it and *verified* it. They have weakened the play by removing a telling example of the subordinated female; but they have verified it unwittingly by extending into the real world the play's thematic concern with the ruthless manipulation of women by men. (Silent *male* characters in the plays are customarily allowed to remain.)

When I had the opportunity to edit *Much Ado about Nothing*, I therefore took great pleasure in restoring Innogen to the text. Just as the apparently dead Hero is eventually resurrected in the play, the silent Innogen (her long-suffering mother) has been deliberately resurrected for this edition.[3] 'The empty vessel makes the greatest sound', says the intelligent Boy in *Henry V*, and, conversely, good acting can accord a character's silence the most eloquent expressiveness. Still waters run deep. I've never forgotten Vivien Leigh's poignant performance as the tongueless Lavinia in Peter Brook's *Titus Andronicus* at Stratford-upon-Avon in 1955. Her eyes, gestures and postures silently uttered resounding eloquence. The stillness was sometimes hieratic; the poignancy offset the horror.

An obvious conclusion follows. Let's bring back to the light of day not only Innogen but all the rest of the editorially-buried humanity in Shakespeare!

Notes:
1. See Appendix A of Roger Warren's edition of *Cymbeline* (Oxford: Oxford University Press, 1998), pp. 265-8. Although the First Folio calls the heroine of *Cymbeline* 'Imogen', this may result from a misreading of Shakespeare's writing. Simon Forman's eye-witness account of the play calls her 'Innogen': that's how he heard it. Furthermore, Holinshed's *Chronicles* (so often consulted by Shakespeare) specify 'Innogen' as the name of the first Queen of Britain. In *Cymbeline*, Innogen is linked to a character called 'Leonatus'; in *Much Ado*, she is linked to Leonato. It all fits!
2. Shakespeare there recycles a joke he had used in *The Taming of the Shrew*, Act 5, scene 1. (Lines 28-9 in my edition.)
3. *Much Ado about Nothing* (Ware: Wordsworth, 2003).

15

Banish the Sentimentalist's Claudio!
The Puzzle of *Much Ado about Nothing*, Act 5, scene 3.

Out goes Shakespeare, in comes the editor! Too often, in the traditional published canon of Shakespeare's works, we find that editors have succumbed to an egoistic vice. They have deleted or altered Shakespearian material that they dislike in order to create new effects of their own which (naturally) they regard as superior. Various respected texts of *Much Ado about Nothing* provide two remarkable examples of this procedure.

In the previous chapter, I showed how Innogen, Hero's mother, has traditionally been excised from the text by possibly male-chauvinistic editors. That's bad enough; but *Much Ado about Nothing* provides a second example of editorial meddling, and this one definitely thwarts Shakespeare's clear and intelligent intentions.

In what is customarily designated scene 3 of Act 5, the setting is a monumental tomb in a churchyard. What takes place here is a ritual of mourning for the apparently dead Hero; and, according to numerous modern texts of the play, the penitent Claudio is central to that ritual. In a greatly-respected Arden text, for example, we find that the people who enter are Claudio, Don Pedro, three or four men with tapers, Balthasar and a group of musicians. Claudio reads from a scroll the following poem of lamentation for Hero:

> 'Done to death by slanderous tongues
>   Was the Hero that here lies:
> Death, in guerdon of her wrongs,
>   Gives her fame which never dies:
> So the life that died with shame
> Lives in death with glorious fame.'
>   [*Hangs up the scroll.*]
> Hang thou there upon the tomb,

68

>   Praising her when I am dumb.[1]

He calls for music; Balthasar then sings the song 'Pardon, goddess of the night', and Claudio rounds it off by saying: 'Now unto thy bones good night! / Yearly will I do this rite.' Bidding farewell to each other, the men then go their separate ways.

Morally, all this seems very satisfactory: the penitent Claudio is mourning Hero as he should. Numerous other editors arrange the speeches so that Claudio similarly dominates the proceedings. For instance, such acclaimed editions as Peter Alexander's, the *Riverside Shakespeare*, the Oxford *Complete Works* and the commodious *Norton Shakespeare* let Claudio read that poem and invoke the song (usually sung not by Balthasar but by 'three or four with tapers'). In various productions for stage and screen, Claudio's voice is tremulous with grief, and he wipes away his tears. A 1993 staging at Edinburgh even allowed Hero to eavesdrop on his penitence, so that the eventual reconciliation would seem more credible.

If, however, we go back to Shakespeare, we discover a very different scene. The most authoritative version of *Much Ado about Nothing* is the Quarto of 1600, the earliest printed text of the play. That text appears to derive from Shakespeare's 'foul papers': in other words, from an untidy manuscript by the playwright. In this 1600 Quarto, we find that the stage-directions and speech-headings do not actually specify Balthasar and the musicians, who featured in that Arden text. Furthermore, and crucially, in the Quarto, the person who reads the 'Done to death' poem is not Claudio at all. That poem is read by an anonymous 'Lord'. Then follows the song, evidently rendered by the 'three or foure' taper-bearers mentioned in the stage-directions. Immediately after the song, we find the words 'Now vnto thy bones good night, yeerely will I doe this right.' These words are allocated, however, not to Claudio but to '*Lo.*', in other words, a Lord. A sceptic might say, 'But that's only the Quarto text. What about the First Folio, 1623?'. Well, the First Folio has very small variants in spelling and punctuation, but otherwise is the same. The speeches are allocated to the same people. Just as in the Quarto,

Claudio has little to say: not thirteen lines (as in those modern texts) but just five lines in the whole scene.

You can now perceive what numerous editors have been conspiring to do. They have been replacing Shakespearian material that they don't like with editorial material that they prefer. The standard editorial adaptation, in giving the poem and its ensuing couplet to Claudio, makes him more prominent and modifies his character. He now is an eloquently penitent mourner for the supposedly dead Hero. Editors thus push the characterisation and the play's morality firmly towards conventionality of a sentimental kind. So here is an obvious puzzle. If you are editing this play, should you support this academic custom, or should you seek to preserve the authentic script?

From that somewhat tendentious phrasing ('academic' versus 'authentic'? – no contest!), you can infer my answer. When I edited *Much Ado about Nothing* for Wordsworth Classics, I rebelled against the sentimental tradition. What was good enough for Shakespeare was good enough for me. I respected the original speech-allocations of the scene. Such fidelity, while preserving the elegiac qualities, seemed to heighten the ritual's strangeness. And you can see that a new feature emerged. Out went the traditional soft and sentimental version of Claudio in this scene, while the original cooler and more reticent Claudio reappeared; and this character is consistent with the rather callous and calculating character seen previously. He had *wooed Hero by proxy*. At the dance in Act 1, Don Pedro had won her over for him. Now, in Act 5, Claudio, with ironic consistency, *mourns her by proxy*. An anonymous lord must lament the 'slanderous tongues' which have supposedly killed her. And the worst of those tongues was Claudio's.

The authentic scene of lamentation now fits the pattern of Claudio's characterisation: though he was quick to denounce Hero, the play repeatedly depicts him as strangely detached. When we had seen Claudio previously, after the supposed death of Hero, instead of expressing remorse at his part in her decease, he had joined Don Pedro in jesting that Benedick would soon be married to an adulterous wife. There we saw levity rather than penitence. Some time afterwards, Hero's innocence having been established, Claudio will swiftly agree to make amends – by marrying speedily a woman whom he has never seen (Leonato's 'niece') and does not know. Thus, having been ruthless in wrongly denouncing Hero as a whore, he is now unflinchingly willing to undertake a bizarrely loveless marriage. The original scene at the monument, with its reticent Claudio, fits this sequence far better than the sentimentalised version of that scene.

Editors have tried to make Claudio better than he really is. In doing so, they have thwarted the intentions of Shakespeare, who clearly designed a play which (for all its comic levity) repeatedly offers bitter-sweet, harsh and jarring effects. In *Much Ado about Nothing*, Shakespeare is already moving into the genre of the 'Problem Comedy'. In that genre, he depicts markedly unheroic heroes: unlikeable male protagonists. *Much Ado*'s Claudio partly resembles his namesake, the changeably callow Claudio of *Measure for Measure*. Strikingly, moreover, the Claudio of *Much Ado* resembles the haughtily cruel and fickle Bertram of *All's Well That Ends Well*: another young man who is prepared not only to slander and spurn the woman who loves him, but also, after her supposed death, to accept in marriage an unknown female. Here Shakespeare is giving tips to Ibsen, Shaw and Brecht. 'Alienation effects'? Shakespeare revelled in them.

In short: the tradition of 'softening' the Claudio of *Much Ado*'s Act 5, scene 3, displays sentimentality and fails to understand Shakespeare's complex and evolving intentions. Too often, conventional editorial notions of comedy have displaced Shakespeare's interest in the problematic and the disturbing. In future, let us trust the Quarto: the Bard knows best!

Note:
1. *Much Ado about Nothing*, ed. A. R. Humphreys (London: Methuen, 1981), 5.3.3-11, pp. 210-11.

16

'Dauphin' or 'Dolphin' in *Henry V*?

Virtually all editors of Shakespeare's *Henry V* use the word 'Dauphin' to refer to the French King's son and heir. This custom is so widespread and long-established that the reader may well assume that that is the title which Shakespeare himself employed.

Of course, its pronunciation may cause us to hesitate. Should we attempt to be politically correct and pronounce 'dauphin' in modern French style, or should we be patriotically courageous and anglicise it ('dáw-fin')? Either way, we probably trust the editors to copy Shakespeare's spelling of the word. But this trust would be misplaced.

In all the earliest texts of *Henry V*, namely the Quartos of Shakespeare's time and the First Folio of 1623, the word appears as 'Dolphin'. It is used numerous times, and repeatedly it is 'Dolphin'. Yes, the same as the name of the marine mammal. And those texts should provide the foundations of all subsequent editions.

What *are* the editors playing at? They probably think that Shakespeare's usage looks quaint and absurd, whereas 'Dauphin' is familiar, customary and respectable. But they are being anachronistic. The *Oxford English Dictionary* shows that, from Mediæval times to the late 17th century, the common spellings were 'daulphin', 'daulphyn', 'dolphyn' and 'dolphin'. In 1494, for instance, Fabyan's *Chronicles* said that 'the dolphyn of Yven [...] solde his dolphynage vnto the Frenshe kynge'. Cotgrave's *Dictionarie* (1611) refers to 'Daulphin de France. *The Dolphin, or eldest sonne of France*'.[1] The title derived from 'a proper name *Delphinus* (the same word as the name of the fish [*sic*])', the *O.E.D.* reports, and in Mediæval French it sometimes appears as 'Daulphin' and 'Dalfin'. The marine mammal's name seems to have been the same as (and indeed the source of) the prince's title, deriving from the Latin *delphinus* and ultimately the Greek *delphis*. So 'Dolphin' is etymologically sound and is no parody of that title. The dolphin was sometimes considered the highest in the 'chain of being' among the fishes, the dogfish being one of the lowest. In legend, the dolphin is intelligent and benign: famously, the rescuer of Arion.

You can see that there ensues an obvious puzzle for a present-day editor of *Henry V*. Should one be conventional, unsurprising and traditional, do what so many other editors have done, and use the respectable 'Dauphin'; or should one be true to the original period and faithful to the Shakespearian texts (which, almost certainly, incorporate Shakespeare's own preferred spelling) and use 'Dolphin'? In my view, the answer is clear; so my edition of *Henry V* employs 'Dolphin' throughout. One reason is simply sensual.

At my Grammar School, long ago, the English masters urged the students to appreciate Shakespeare's euphonies. In particular, we were urged to trace the patterns of alliteration and assonance in the poetry. Now, in the following passage, part of a defiant speech by Henry, consider what would happen if, as is customarily the case, editors were to change this 'Dolphin' to 'Dauphin'.

> But I will rise there with so full a glory
> That I will dazzle all the eyes of France,
> Yea, strike the Dolphin blind to look on us;
> And tell the pleasant prince, this mock of his
> Hath turned his balls to gun-stones, and his soul
> Shall stand sore chargèd for the wasteful vengeance...[1]

You can hear how the quoted lines work. The 'ol' of 'Dolphin' resonates with 'will', 'full', 'will dazzle all', 'tell', 'balls', 'soul' and 'wasteful'; the 'i' of '-phin' assonates with 'will'(twice), 'prince', 'this' and the repeated 'his'; and the 'n' of 'phin' recurs no fewer than twelve times. Editors who substitute 'Dauphin' (and thereby solicit current French pronunciation) rip the centre from this rich network of alliterative and assonantal effects. The 'ol', the English 'i' sound and the English 'n' sound vanish. You might proceed to consider the aural damage that is inflicted when the First Folio's

'Harflew', 'Callice' and disyllabic 'Roan' are changed by well-meaning editors (as is customary) to 'Harfleur', 'Calais' and 'Rouen'. Again, in *Henry VI, Part 1*, Talbot furiously denounces La Pucelle ('the Maiden', Joan of Arc) and the French Prince thus:

> Puzzel or Pucelle, dolphin or dogfish,
> Your hearts I'll stamp out with my horse's heels...

This word-play, linking Pucelle, via 'Puzzel', to whore, and linking the dolphin, highest of the fishes, with the dogfish, one of the lowest, would be marred in a play which termed the Frenchman 'Dauphin'.

So you see that this not just a matter of a few words in *Henry V*: there are implications for the whole of Shakespeare. Think of the difference in *Macbeth* when the First Folio's 'weyward' and 'weyard' sisters are editorially modernised to 'weird' sisters. ('Weyward' suggests 'unnatural, wilfully perverse', which precisely fits their chant 'Fair is foul and foul is fair'; whereas 'weird' suggests the less precise 'strange, eldritch, peculiar'.) Again, think of the recurrent metrical damage which is inflicted on *The Tempest* when the Folio's 'Millaine' (always accented on the *first* syllable) is emended as the modern 'Milan' (always accented on the *second* syllable). To take just one instance: 'Thy father was the Duke of Míllaine and / A prince of power'. That sounds fine; but modernise it as 'Thy father was the Duke of Milán and / A prince of power', and immediately the metre becomes awkwardly irregular, while the conjunction of 'Milán' with 'and' (making 'an-an') is jarring.[3]

In short, if we really value the poetry of Shakespeare, let us get rid of these needless modernisations of his diction which mar his music. Let the euphonies sing! We, today, may never utter all his terms and names *exactly* as he would have uttered them,[4] but that's no excuse for modernisations which constitute aural vandalism.

Notes:

1. Randle Cotgrave: *A Dictionarie of the French and English Tongues* [1611] (reprinted; Menston: Scolar Press, 1968).
2. *Henry V*, ed. Cedric Watts (Ware: Wordsworth, 2000), 1.2.279-84.
3. I return later to this matter, in the 'wise or wife' puzzle.
4. The British Library's CD, *Shakespeare's Original Pronunciation* (2012), is helpful.

17

Brutus: Hypocritical Stoic?

To lose a wife *once* may be regarded as a misfortune; to lose her *twice* looks like carelessness. The earliest extant text of *Julius Cæsar* appears in the First Folio (1623); and, in its version of what is now Act 4, scene 2, something peculiar happens. The death of Portia, Brutus's wife, is announced not once but twice. And, even more peculiarly, Brutus's responses differ dramatically. Why is this?

During the quarrelsome exchanges in this scene, Cassius, who never condescends to let his arguments be adulterated by tact, reproaches Brutus for failing to exemplify the Stoical philosophy that he supposedly has espoused. 'I am sick of many griefs', Brutus has said. Cassius remarks critically:

> Of your philosophy you make no use,
> If you give place to accidental evils.[1]

In other words: 'You are not practising your particular philosophy of life, if you let fortuitous woes afflict you like this.' He knows that Brutus is a Stoic, and Stoics strive to be unmoved by circumstances and to achieve equanimity.

Brutus responds: 'No man bears sorrow better. Portia is dead.' In just three words, he thus announces that his beloved wife has died. (There is no doubt that she was 'beloved': the mutuality of the love of Brutus and Portia was strongly established in Act 2, scene 1.) Cassius, understandably shocked, exclaims: 'How scaped I killing, when I crossed you so?': that is to say, 'Now that I know of your bereavement, I can see that when I criticised you I was so tactless that I was lucky not to be killed by you.' (He realises that Brutus must indeed be truly stoical.) Brutus then explains that Portia has committed suicide. She had pined for Brutus and had grieved that Antony and Octavius, his foes, were gaining strength. Distraught, she has 'swallowed fire' to die. (Plutarch's *Lives*, Shakespeare's main source for the play, says that when Portia was ill, she chose to die rather than languish in pain; consequently, she put burning coals in her mouth and kept it shut, so that she died of suffocation.) 'O ye immortal gods!', responds Cassius; but Brutus, in a classically stoical response, says: 'Speak no more of her. – Give me a bowl of wine.'

That dramatic exchange spans lines 195-208 of Act 4, scene 2. What ensues, however, is peculiar. Five lines later (at line 213), Titinius and Messala enter. During the ensuing conversation, Brutus expresses his suspicion that Messala is concealing what he knows of Portia. Messala, after asking Brutus to bear the news 'like a Roman, responds: 'For certain she is dead, and by strange manner.' Brutus briskly comments:

> Why, farewell, Portia. – We must die, Messala:
> By meditating that she must die once,
> I have the patience to endure it now.

Coolly tutorial in style: after bidding her farewell, Brutus gives a concise lesson to Messala, which may be paraphrased thus: 'Having reflected that she was bound to die at one time or another, I am braced for this event.' Duly impressed, Messala replies: 'Even so great men great losses should endure'. He approves the remarkably stoical – or seemingly callous – response.

This is very odd. The same event, as we see, is announced in two different ways, and Brutus receives it each time as if it were the *first* time. One way of explaining the second occurrence is to say that Brutus's hypocrisy is being revealed. Although he already knows that Portia is dead, he pretends to Messala that he is learning the news for the first time, so that he can make a practised stoical reply, thus impressing Messala and winning his approval. In that case, however, Cassius would hardly have said, as he does,

> I have as much of this in art as you,
> But yet my nature could not bear it so.

This means: 'In theory, I'm a Stoic, too; but, in practice, I could not have carried off the matter as coolly as you have done: nature would have defeated lore.' It seems most unlikely that he would use these words cynically, to endorse any deception of Messala by Brutus. In the case of such a deception, a more likely response from Cassius, who is a touchy fellow, would be a sharply critical protest at the calculated duplicity. I imagine such protesting pentameters as these:

> You play the Stoic to impress your friend,
> But make me puke. *Our* friendship's at an end!' [*Exit*].

Another way of explaining the repetition, and one favoured by numerous editors, is to speculate as follows. Perhaps, after writing one version, Shakespeare changed his mind and wrote an alternative version; and, although one was supposed to be cancelled, it has remained in print alongside the other. We know that there is precedent for such duplication. In *Love's Labour's Lost*, we find both revised and unrevised versions of a passage in Act 4, scene 3, and of another passage in Act 5, scene 2. *Romeo and Juliet*, as we have seen, offers another example.

Obviously enough, however, this explanatory hypothesis creates a new problem. Editors have to decide *which* of the two *Julius Cæsar* passages is the one that Shakespeare meant to cancel. Curiously, *both* look like later insertions into the scene. If lines 193-208 are ignored, these being the lines in which the death of Portia is announced by Brutus to Cassius, the action and dialogue run fluently. Lucius is asked to supply a bowl of wine, and Brutus proceeds to drink a toast to his renewed friendship with Cassius. What happens if, alternatively, we ignore lines 231-45, which present the second announcement of Portia's death? Once again, the action and dialogue run fluently. After Messala has noted that Cicero is dead, Brutus aptly comments, 'Well, to our work alive.' There is no sense of an awkward transition.

So, if you are staging the play, you find that have at least four options here. 1. You keep both the passages. Then the audience sees unexpected deviousness on the part of Brutus: he seems cunningly manipulative. Option 2. Cut lines 231-45 (the Messala entry), thus accentuating the relatively gentle Brutus and his reconciliation with the now-sympathetic Cassius. 3. Cut lines 193-208, to show Brutus as toughly, almost ruthlessly, stoical. 4. You delete *both* the disputed passages. This way you don't *solve* the puzzle; you *dis*solve it, while saving time. Directors almost always find it necessary to excise passages from Shakespeare's plays; and audiences, hastening out for a drink or for the journey home, seldom complain.

Nevertheless, in my edition of *Julius Cæsar*, I chose the first option: thus I was true to the First Folio. I then, democratically, offered readers their own choice, by means of the textual notes which explained the alternatives, so that the readers could weigh the options and mentally stage their preferred solution.

If I were physically staging the play, however, I would probably adopt the option which seems, on the whole, to be the most logical and most consistent with the broad context. I think that passage 231-45 depicts Brutus as too severe, and that the earlier passage represents Shakespeare's improvement. That earlier and more elaborate treatment is true to the relatively mild character of Brutus (who there concedes the greatness of his sorrow), and aptly completes the reconciliation of the leaders. The integration of the fuller version is completed with Cassius' interjection, 'Portia, art thou gone?', at line 216. There, even after the arrival of Titnius and Messala, Cassius is still musing on the shocking news, dismay surging afresh; so that Brutus has to curb him with 'No more, I pray you': a finely realistic and psychologically telling instance of the interplay between these two contrasting allies.

What this puzzle demonstrates is that, when we are dealing with Shakespearian material, different solutions are appropriate in different situations. The editor has a duty to his readers to make clear the nature of the crux, so that each reader may assess the alternatives, enacting them on the portable stage between the ears. A director of the play, in contrast, has a duty to co-ordinate the textual material in the light of his or her interpretation of the plot, characterisation, themes, etc. In that case, the democratic choices for the audiences are generated largely by their awareness of the 'mutual jars' – the collisions and discrepancies – between different productions. Let multiplicity thrive!

Note:
1. The quoted material corresponds to that in my edition of *Julius Cæsar* (Ware: Wordsworth, 2004), and line numbers refer to this edition. The basis of its text was, of course, the First Folio's version of the play, but I editorially modernised (where it seemed necessary and appropriate to do so), the First Folio's spelling and punctuation.

18

Hamlet or *Hamleth*?

Various puzzles in *Hamlet* result from the mixture of old and new. Sophisticated Shakespeare was adapting relatively primitive material, and a complex muddle emerged.

One salutary name for such a muddle is 'a palimpsest'. That's the term for an inscribed object on which older writing shows through the newer, often yielding a confusing result. *Hamlet* is a vast palimpsest.

We are frequently told that the original story of Hamlet (or Amlothi or Amlotha or Amleth, or kindred names) emerged in ancient, pre-Christian times, in the era of Norse sagas. It was transmitted to Shakespeare from mediaeval Scandinavia via Saxo Grammaticus's *Historiae Danicae* (written around A.D. 1200), via the *Histoires Tragiques* of Belleforest (*circa* 1570) and via a lost play probably written by Thomas Kyd (*circa* 1590). Almost predictably, muddles ensued.

The Bard did what he could to modernise the legend and make it more subtle, sensitive and realistic. But parts of the earlier barbaric plot and the earlier violent Amleth remain, and the result is inconsistency. Hamlet himself is a hybrid: partly a brooding philosopher ('To be or not to be...'), partly a ruthless avenger ('Now could I drink hot blood'). Aptly, therefore, the role has been performed by two contrasting actors simultaneously: twins, Anthony and David Meyer, in a remarkable televised performance (1976).

The Prince is sensitively generous to Horatio and the players, but callous to Polonius, Ophelia and the doomed Rosencrantz and Guildenstern. Like Aladdin's in a pantomime, his primary motivation is often not moral or psychological, but *inherited and literary*: he does certain things because they are what the legendary Amleth traditionally did.

Partly, our Hamlet is the puppet of the past. The feigned madness, the slaughter of an eavesdropper in the Queen's bedchamber, the callous disposal of that corpse; the voyage to England, the ruthless despatch of two escorts by changing the letter they carry: all these features can be found in the ancient legend.

Thus, our Hamlet lurches between civilised reflections and harsh conduct, because the likeable modern character is repeatedly being manipulated by the old plot and is obliged at times to mimic the nastiness of his ancient namesake.

Even when Hamlet's feigned madness modulates into apparent manic-depression, there's precedent in Amleth, whose feigned idiocy was a halfway house between melancholy and genuine dementia. What's more, 'Amleth' means 'Dimwit', so the most intelligent character in Shakespeare bears a name recalling a stigma of stupidity – though it was ironic even in the case of the crafty ancient avenger, who wasn't as crazy as he purported to be.

The play's historical and cultural allusions are exuberantly palimpsestic. The wildly inconsistent historical contexts that the play invokes reflect the legend's longevity. Claudius (in Act 4, scene 3)[1] specifies that the action takes place during the era of the Danegeld, i.e. between the tenth and twelfth centuries, when a humbled England paid financial tribute to Denmark: that's why he is confident that the English court will be obliged to receive Hamlet and carry out Claudius's command to kill him. England is the 'faithful tributary', we are reminded in Act 5, scene 2. The wrathful Hamlet Senior, in his armour, seems to belong to the Middle Ages. We recall him on the ice, zealously performing as you or the editors direct him: sometimes he is thumping his leaded 'pole-axe' down to emphasise a point; sometimes, instead, he is smiting 'Polacks' (Polish warriors) as they ride on their sledges. Either way, he's a martial figure from the legendary past: he has even won territory by slaying Fortinbras Senior in single combat. Nevertheless, in the play's climactic scene, the duellists use rapiers, which became fashionable in the late 16th century. Furthermore, the text refers explicitly to the child-players who flourished around 1600 (Act 2, scene 2). Hamlet's admirable advocacy of realism in acting (Act 3, scene 2) anticipates even later periods, conceivably including the 'Method' acting of the 1950s. Certainly the ideal he describes evokes James Dean rather than Donald Wolfit, or, subsequently, Simon Russell Beale rather than Alan Rickman.

The Ghost's eschatology is Roman Catholic, for it specifies Purgatory; yet Hamlet, at thirty years of age a remarkably mature student at Wittenberg (noted centre of Protestantism), variously expresses vengefulness, piety, agnosticism and radical scepticism ('there is nothing either good or bad, but thinking makes it so').

In one of Hamlet's soliloquies, Shakespeare finely meets the challenge of resolving the main conflicts which divide and rive the Prince. Here he resolves them locally by portraying Hamlet as a coherent character voicing a moral and psychological division without consciously perceiving the extent of it. That is the soliloquy beginning 'How all occasions do inform against me' (Act 4, scene 4). Regrettably, some editors (by prioritising the Folio text, which lacks it) relegate the speech to an appendix. Yet this soliloquy resolves psychologically the division generated largely by the work's heritage. The words express a clear conflict between two ethics: one being the consciously-voiced, old, inherited revenge ethic; the other being the subconscious, modern, humane ethic. I quote the last two-thirds:

> Examples gross as earth exhort me.
> Witness this army of such mass and charge,
> Led by a delicate and tender prince,
> Whose spirit with divine ambition puffed
> Makes mouths at the invisible event,
> Exposing what is mortal and unsure
> To all that fortune, death and danger dare,
> Even for an egg-shell. Rightly to be great
> Is not to stir without great argument,
> But greatly to find quarrel in a straw
> When honour's at the stake. How stand I then,
> That have a father killed, a mother stained,
> Excitements of my reason and my blood,

> And let all sleep, while to my shame I see
> The imminent death of twenty thousand men,
> That for a fantasy and trick of fame
> Go to their graves like beds, fight for a plot
> Whereon the numbers cannot try the cause,
> Which is not tomb enough and continent
> To hide the slain? O, from this time forth,
> My thoughts be bloody, or be nothing worth!

Here, muddle is transmuted into a plausibly divided self, most tellingly in the declaration with the 'erroneous negative'. When arguing that he should act bloodily and decisively, Hamlet says: 'Rightly to be great / Is not to stir without great argument'. What he consciously *intends* to say is that a truly great man needs no strong justification before going into action. But there is an erroneous 'not' in his phrasing: the intended sense requires only 'Is to stir without great argument'. What he *actually* says, instead, is the opposite: that a great man should *not* stir without strong justification. By inserting that 'not', Shakespeare generates proleptically a 'Freudian slip' revealing Hamlet's inner misgivings about hasty violence that lacks an ample basis.

This sense of repressed humanity, of a civilised and modern resistance to violence, which breaks though the surface, opposing the destructive will, is also expressed with keen intelligence in the imagery of that soliloquy. Hamlet declares that a truly great man could find sufficient pretext for violence 'in a straw'. In 'a straw'? Does that imply greatness or idiocy? Twenty thousand men, he proceeds to say, admirably die for 'a fantasy and trick of fame'. But can it really be admirable that thousands of human beings perish for a mere fancy, for a 'trick' (trivial gain, or quirk, or deceit) of fame? And the area conquered in battle will be a plot of land 'Which is not tomb enough and continent / To hide the slain' – which is not large enough to bury and conceal the corpses of the combatants! As Kipling could tell us, that would be as unwise as committing British troops to a war in Afghanistan.

So, although Hamlet's reflections here lead him to vow to be 'bloody' henceforth, all those ambiguities in his 'How all occasions' speech prepare us for further procrastination on his part. The large-scale palimpsest of the plot here generates a characterisation which is not *contradictorily* palimpsestic, but *paradoxically* so. A seemingly contradictory characterisation is now resolved in a divided character, a living paradox: a credible self in conflict. And when Hamlet does eventually strike out against Claudius, it's after he finds himself lethally caught in an ambush: the victim, not the victimiser. Accepting 'providence', he has stoically entered the duel, largely expelling the character of his vengeful legendary predecessor who, after murdering numerous revellers, had cynically granted his doomed opponent a useless sword (nailed to its scabbard), thereby ambushing the villain. The contrasting Shakespearian ambush-plot finally resolves the Prince's moral dilemma. And that's partly why, in our moral judgements, we treat Hamlet so leniently. Our Hamlet becomes the victim of lethal cunning: he has sloughed off, at last, his legendary ancestor who was the callous wielder of such craftiness.

With the help of editors, of gifted actors, and of directors who (taking Hamlet's advice – 'It shall to the barber's') cut the text, superb order often emerges from the muddle of Shakespeare's drama and its diverse early scripts. All such activity was astutely prophesied by the Player King when declaring 'Our thoughts are ours, their ends none of our own.'

Nevertheless, if we seek a title which is true to the play's nature, this tragedy could be called, not *Hamlet* (too modern), not *Amleth* (too ancient), but *Hamleth*: a concise palimpsestic name for the elaborately palimpsestic drama and character.

Note:
1. Textual citations are from *Hamlet*, ed. Cedric Watts (Ware: Wordsworth, 2002).

19

Malvolio's Revenge: What is It?

In *Twelfth Night*, the last line to be uttered by the vanquished Malvolio is, of course, 'I'll be revenged on the whole pack of you!'. Its tone will depend on our imaginations or, if we are listening to the words in a stage, screen or radio production, on the interpretation by the actor or director. The tone could be coldly malevolent, courageously defiant or tearfully hysterical. Influenced by a particularly memorable performance by Laurence Olivier, I imagine a wailing, howling tone. I used to think that the threat was pitiably and half-comically empty, in the same category as Lear's desperate cry, '

> I will do such things –
> What they are yet I know not, but they shall be/
> The terrors of the earth!'

But is Malvolio's threat *really* empty?

I was wrong to think it so. Eventually, Malvolio is no fool – and no Fool either.

Malvolio has been incarcerated, and driven near to madness by being treated as a madman. Certainly, he deserves some mockery for his censoriousness and his vain romantic ambition; but he is punished excessively. He has indeed, as he claims and Olivia confirms, been 'notoriously abused'. Like other readers and theatre-goers, I have long felt that his downfall is so distasteful, as he changes from butt of humour to victim of cruelty, that he deserves a chance to strike back.

Before that, entertainingly enough, he had been transformed into a buffoonish deluded lover. He'd been obliged to utter, unwittingly, filthy double meanings: 'her very c's, her u's, and her t's, and thus makes she her great P's'. (Here 'c', 'u' and 't' suggest 'cut', meaning 'cunt', while 'P's' evokes 'pees', flows of urine.) He'd been persuaded to appear cross-gartered and grinning inanely; and he has been thoroughly humiliated.

Nevertheless, if his desire for Olivia has been mixed with folly and delusion, his plight is not entirely different from that of Orsino, desiring Olivia but attracted to Cesario; or from that of Olivia, infatuated with a messenger who is a woman disguised, so that the homo-erotic and the hetero-erotic are teasingly intermingled.

Repeatedly in this play, love is odd and veers towards madness. Sebastian finds himself being wooed by a woman he has only just met, and reflects that either 'I am mad, / Or else the lady's mad'. Nevertheless, he gladly accepts Olivia's importunity to wedlock; and she has swiftly abandoned her pledge to mourn her brother for seven years in seclusion. When Orsino learns that Olivia loves Cesario, he promptly becomes murderously vengeful:

> Come, boy, with me; my thoughts are ripe in mischief:
> I'll sacrifice the lamb that I do love,
> To spite a raven's heart within a dove.

Here, love resembles lethal lunacy. Within a few minutes, when Orsino learns that Olivia has married Sebastian and that Cesario is really a woman, a brisk amatory conversion takes place: now Orsino claims the emergent Viola as his bride. (What *does* she see in him?) While wishing them luck, we may recall Feste's remark that 'fools are as like husbands as pilchards are to herrings – the husband's the bigger'. We gradually recognise that Malvolio, duped as lover and incarcerated as madman, serves as scapegoat for the follies of love which are so widespread in his world.

Early in the play, Malvolio rebukes the revellers, and earns the famous retort from Sir Toby: 'Dost thou think, because thou art virtuous, there shall be no more cakes and ale?'. Obviously, however, without the activities of working people, including Malvolio the steward, there would be no 'cakes and ale' for such parasitic consumers as Sir Toby Belch and Sir Andrew Aguecheek. When Malvolio upbraids them for their drunken noisiness, he is only doing his job, after all; and they are behaving boorishly in what is supposed to be a house of mourning.

In short, I think that Malvolio, downcast near the end of *Twelfth Night*, is entitled to a measure of revenge. Eventually, his revenge *may* take *one* form and *will* take *two* forms.

The final marriage to cement the love-relationships cannot take place until Malvolio is pacified and the matter of the sea-captain is resolved; and the key to that resolution is held by Malvolio. As Duke Orsino says of the departed steward:

> Pursue him, and entreat him to a peace:
> He hath not told us of the captain yet.
> When that is known, and golden time convents,
> A solemn combination shall be made
> Of our dear souls.

Olivia expected the steward, who had sued the captain, to 'enlarge' (free) him. The implication is that, since Malvolio is responsible for the captain's incarceration, only Malvolio, by withdrawing his lawsuit against him, can effect his liberation, which, in view of Viola's indebtedness to that gallant seafarer, must surely be a condition of her marriage to Orsino. Evidently the captain, as she had requested, had first introduced her to the moody Duke. Therefore, if Malvolio wishes to live up to his name ('Ill-Will', 'Malevolent'), he can do so by maintaining his lawsuit and preventing the climactic nuptials.

In any case, symbolically, Malvolio would be avenged historically. During the Elizabethan and Jacobean periods, the Puritans saw the theatre as a den of iniquity, and denounced the actors as corruptors of public morals. Predictably, then, in plays of that era, puritanical characters are mocked as killjoys or depicted as hypocrites: Angelo in *Measure for Measure* comes to mind, accompanied by Ananias, Tribulation and Zeal-of-the-Land Busy in Ben Jonson's *The Alchemist* and *Bartholomew Fair*. When, through the Civil Wat of the 1640s, the Puritans came to power, they promptly closed the theatres. In *Twelfth Night*, Feste, mocking puritanical Malvolio, says 'And thus the whirligig of time brings in his revenges'; but the same 'whirligig of time' will thus bring in, symbolically, the revenge of Malvolio upon Feste.

Furthermore, Malvolio is avenged on a grand scale – by his theatrical destiny. As critics and audiences have long recognised, he is the most interesting character in the play. Malvolio is the plum rôle; he's the star turn. He is variously aloof, authoritative, critical, besotted, idiotic, victimised, confused and humiliated. His range of attitudes, appearances and feelings is so great that it makes the other characters look relatively two-dimensional. From Macklin and Kemble to Donald Sinden, Richard Briers, Patrick Stewart, Derek Jacobi, Stephen Fry and subsequent performers, numerous actors have excelled in the rôle, overshadowing those colleagues playing Orsino or Olivia or even Viola. Like Shylock, Malvolio is a joyless character, an attractor of derision, who yet wins from audiences enough sympathy to approach – however gauchely – tragic stature. Critical of parasites, Malvolio is repeatedly guilty of theft: he steals the show.

So we needn't feel sorry for him. In theatrical history, as the most fascinating character in *Twelfth Night*, Malvolio has long achieved his vengeance.

Note:
Quotations from *King Lear* and *Twelfth Night* are from my editions (Ware: Wordsworth, 2001 and 2004 respectively).

20

The Puzzle of the 'Willow Song' in *Othello*.

In *Othello*, on the fatal night, as Desdemona (with Emilia's help) is preparing for bed, she sings a song with the refrain 'Sing willow, willow, willow'. Or does she?

The problem is that Desdemona's song is present in the earliest text of *Othello*, the First Quarto (1622), but absent from the First Folio text (1623). As we have noted, Heminge and Condell, who assembled the First Folio, had worked with Shakespeare and knew how the plays had actually been performed when Shakespeare was involved as an actor and (as investor in the company of players) in producing the works. Indeed, being a script-writer and practical man of the theatre, Shakespeare must intermittently have functioned as a director of plays, even if the term 'director' was not, at that time, employed for that functionary. Therefore, scholars believe that whereas the Quarto text of *Othello* represents an early script, the First Folio text represents the version of the play that was actually performed in the theatre in those days. The work had evolved, being trimmed in various ways for various purposes.

So here's an obvious puzzle for present-day editors and directors. Should the 'willow' song be retained in texts and productions today, thus respecting the Shakespearian text of the First Quarto, or should it be deleted, thus respecting the First Folio and the theatrical practice of Shakespeare's day?

The argument for omitting it is obvious. A performance of the full Quarto text of *Othello* would be too lengthy for the comfort of most playgoers. To reduce the play's length to what is comfortable, cuts are traditionally made to the available *Othello* material. A passage involving a clown's conversation with some musicians customarily goes. (It may be found in Act 3, scene 1, of my Wordsworth edition.) If it goes, you then lose the 'thereby hangs a tale' stuff: a bawdy punning gag about a 'tail' (penis) hanging by a 'wind instrument' (the anus): no great loss. Indeed, if you ask a theatregoer what she or he thinks of the clown in *Othello*, the response is likely to be '*What clown?*'. Nobody seems to grumble about *that* cut, so the principle of cutting the play seems to be generally accepted.

One editorial conjecture to explain the absence of the 'willow' song from the Folio is that the boy who played Desdemona found that his voice was breaking. Another is that the boy was not a good singer, and it was easier to excise the musical piece than to find another boy. Since the Restoration, females have performed the part of Desdemona; but even a female may, of course, be an unsatisfactory singer, causing the song's later temporary deletion. The 'willow' piece requires considerable skill: it's one of those slow Shakespearian songs with a repetitive refrain which, when projected by a weak voice, easily sinks into embarrassing bathos. In this respect, a modern melancholy counterpart is 'Willow, weep for me' (written by Anne Ronell, 1932): moving when sung by Ella Fitzgerald or Nina Simone, vapid when sung by less gifted vocalists.

Certainly, in *Othello*, when Desdemona's 'willow' song is rendered effectively, it can wield tear-forcing power. It becomes an intensely poignant part of a movingly intimate quiet interlude. In the previous scene, Desdemona had been subjected to cruel abuse by her husband. In the next scene, he will murder her. Here we eavesdrop on a swan-song. Furthermore, what is sung is no ordinary ballad of sad love.

The lyrics comment ironically upon the tragic action. In them, the forlorn woman says of her evidently faithless lover: 'Let nobody blame him; his scorn I approve'. The young woman of the lyrics is so loyal and self-sacrificing that she won't let anyone blame her man, though he is clearly at fault. In the next and final scene, when Emilia asks the dying Desdemona who is responsible for the lethal assault on her, Desdemona says: 'Nobody; I myself. Farewell'. The song, therefore, not only contributes to the bitter-sweet atmosphere of the placid interlude in which it occurs; it also relates thematically to the impending murder-scene, and perhaps even prompts the extreme utterance in which Desdemona, dying, lies to protect Othello.

Another irony is that Desdemona had learnt the song from her mother's maid, who used to sing it because her partner had forsaken her – 'and she died singing it'. The lyric's association with death is prophetic of Desdemona's own fate. Desdemona sings it because she has been treated badly by Othello, and fears that he is forsaking her. The mother's maid was called 'Barbary', which suggests both 'Barbara' (a Christian saint's name) and 'The Barbary Coast', the coastline of North Africa, peopled by Moors (Othello's kindred), Berbers, Arabs and others. Perhaps the maid known as Barbary was black, as servants sometimes were in Shakespeare's day.

Indeed, there were so many black people in Elizabethan England that in 1601 Queen Elizabeth herself announced that boat-loads of them were to be collected and deported by Caspar Van Zeuden. During the hostilities between England and Spain, Spanish ships had been seized by English seafarers, and, when they contained black slaves, those slaves had been freed and brought back to England – to the 'annoyance' of Her Majesty's people, according to the Queen's decree. Racism is obviously part of the agenda in *Othello* (even Emilia terms Desdemona's marriage 'a most filthy bargain'), and Shakespeare's stance in this play is predominantly anti-racist. Remarkably so, for that time. Consider, in contrast, the depiction of Aaron, the wicked Moor in Shakespeare's early revenge drama, *Titus Andronicus*, who 'will have his soul black, like his hide'. In the 1930s, some spectators were dismayed to see Othello, played by the black Paul Robeson, kiss Desdemona, played by the white Peggy Ashcroft.

The 'willow' song also makes a feminist point. The previous songs in *Othello* have been divisive and associated with hatred. Iago sang two songs ('And let me the cannikin clink' and 'King Stephen was and-a worthy peer') in order to encourage Cassio to get drunk, so that Cassio would readily descend to drunken brawling with Roderigo and be disgraced. Desdemona's song, in contrast, is one of forgiveness and enduring love.

Of course, feminism, as we have seen, is an explicit part of the play's agenda – strikingly explicit in Emilia's lengthy speech at the end of Act 4, scene 3. She says, for instance:

> But I do think it is their husbands' faults
> If wives do fail [...].
> And have we not affections,
> Desires for sport, and frailty, as men have?
> Then let them use us well; else let them know,
> The ills we do, their ills instruct us so.

In other words, women have the same sexual appetites as men; therefore, if men are unfaithful to women, the women may respond accordingly. What's sauce for the goose is sauce for the gander. Hence, while Desdemona's example suggests that women are more constant and altruistic in love than are men, Emilia's speech suggests that if men set a bad example, women may follow it themselves, being much the same in nature. Many of today's feminists would side with Emilia.

Thus, there are numerous reasons, we see, for retaining the 'Willow' piece. But its absence from the Folio offers us a warning. Keep that song – but only if the player of Desdemona has a good voice. When the song fails, it can fail disastrously. Furthermore, when Shakespeare's plays are performed in truncated form, theatre-goers seldom complain. A full production of *Hamlet* could last for a bum-numbing five hours. Prince Hamlet himself favoured cutting a lengthy text. We could apply his injunction, 'It shall to the barber's', to the script of *Othello*. But let's not take the barber's scissors to Emilia's feminist speech. It offers one of those striking occasions when Shakespeare seems proleptic: indeed, not merely anticipatory but prophetic and 'ahead of his times'. There, he is helping to generate the politics of future years – including ours.

Note:
Quotations from *Othello* are from my edition (Ware: Wordsworth, 2002).

21

Othello: Can Impossibility Increase Empathy?

Chronologically, *Othello* is a notoriously strange play; but its tragic protagonist can seem the most poignantly-moving of all such protagonists in Shakespeare. One puzzle presented by the drama is this: can its temporal peculiarity, which threatens to wreck the plot, paradoxically increase our empathy with the jealous Moor himself?

We know that Shakespeare liked to compress and hasten the sequences of events that he found in his sources. That's natural: a play is usually a more concise and/or co-ordinated form than, say, a chronicle or a meditative poetic narrative. Although the action of Chaucer's *Troilus and Criseyde* extends over years, that of Shakespeare's *Troilus and Cressida* seems to take a few days. Shakespeare's history plays repeatedly compress the historical time-scale: for instance, in *Henry V*, the wedding of Henry V to Katharine of France seems to take place much sooner after the Battle of Agincourt than it did in reality. Shakespeare's feats of compression, however, sometimes caused a temporal split in his material: the 'double time-scheme', which is more common than is usually recognised. You can find it in numerous works, including *Richard II*, *Romeo and Juliet*, *The Merchant of Venice* and *Measure for Measure*.

For example, in *Measure for Measure*, the main dramatic events involving the Duke, Claudio, Isabella and Angelo seem to take only four or five days; but the passage of months is implied by the various 'long time' references, e.g. to the Duke's possible journeying to Rome, Poland or Russia, or to his lengthy period as 'Friar Lodowick', repeatedly visiting Mariana. In *Romeo and Juliet*, similarly, the main action requires merely ninety-four hours, but numerous allusions evoke a span extending between five days and several weeks.(as when, for example, minutes after Romeo's departure from Juliet's bedroom, Lady Capulet promises to send someone to poison Romeo 'in Mantua, / Where that same banished runagate doth live').

My general explanation of such cases is that the rapid *action* depends on a slower *plot*, thus sinking synchronicity. The speedy drama in the foreground has been precipitated by a tardy story in the background.

The most notorious of the double time-schemes is, of course, that in *Othello,* which naturally creates the puzzle of our evident empathy with a protagonist whose plight seems temporally impossible. In the main source-tale, Giraldi Cinthio's crime-story in *Gli Hecatommithi*, the chronology is vague, diffuse and long-term; the action spans years. Shakespeare transforms this unpromisingly episodic and sordid narrative into a powerful, eloquent, intense and rapidly-developing tragedy. *Othello*, though its word-length is far greater than that of the tale, is much tauter as a depiction of events; but temporally, in contrast, it is strikingly problematic.

The play's chronological strangeness was first noted in print by the abrasively argumentative critic, Thomas Rymer, in 1692 (in his *Short View of Tragedy*, which, ironically in the circumstances, bears the date '1693'). We recall how Iago persuades Othello that, since his marriage to Desdemona, she has committed adultery with Cassio not once but on numerous occasions. Various 'long-time' references give the impression that ample time has elapsed for the purpose. These include Iago's story about sleeping with Cassio 'lately' and thus witnessing Cassio's lustful dreaming about his continuing love-relationship with the Moor's wife. Another reference is Bianca's reproachful 'What, keep a week away?' to Cassio, indicating that he, having established himself as a regular client of hers, has resided on Cyprus for considerably longer than a week. Roderigo's increasing impatience and impoverishment add to the sense of 'long time': 'I have wasted myself out of my means', he complains to Iago (Act 4, sc. 2): he has fruitlessly exhausted his funds. Emilia says that Iago has on many occasions importuned her to steal Desdemona's handkerchief. Furthermore, Othello can even allege that Desdemona 'with Cassio hath the act of shame / A thousand times committed'. Sexual stakhanovites might require a couple of months for that total; and, even if we make allowances for the customary exaggerations made by an indignant male, several weeks are implied.

On the other hand, as Rymer recognised, close attention to the unfolding events makes evident the fact that only thirty-three hours or so elapse between the arrival of Desdemona on Cyprus and her death at Othello's hands. Citation of differences between the Julian and Gregorian calendars cannot overcome this difficulty, which is a matter not of dates but of temporal adequacy, a problem not of numbers but of durations.

Consider the facts. On the first night together after their marriage, Desdemona is in bed with Othello in Venice, and they are disturbed by the hue and cry instigated by Iago, aided by Roderigo. On their second night together, they are in Cyprus, and are disturbed by the drunken brawl involving Cassio and Roderigo: again, Iago is the instigator. On their third night, Desdemona dies. (Peculiarly, and as if to accentuate the problem, Desdemona, Othello and Cassio sail in three separate vessels from Venice to Cyprus: thus Desdemona could not have enjoyed Cassio's company during the voyage.) There simply has not been time for the lengthy adulterous relationship to have occurred; and it is definitely adultery – not pre-marital intercourse – which is repeatedly specified. Iago slanders Desdemona and reiterates the allegation of adultery when he asserts that Venetian women 'let God see the pranks / They dare not show their husbands'.

Thomas Rymer curtly remarks:

> The *Audience* must suppose a great many bouts [i.e. adulterous encounters], to make the plot operate. They must deny their senses, to reconcile it to common sense: or make it any way consistent, and hang together.[1]

Therefore, claims Rymer, the plot founders on gross illogicality.

Well, it would do, if we maintained a precise chronological awareness. But audiences seem to accommodate the illogicality. Being so caught up in the moment-by-moment development of the accelerating action, the spectators seem to accept imaginatively, if not to reconcile, the logically irreconcilable. But audiences, though accommodating, do not 'deny their senses': they naturally register the audible and visible chronological information put before them; and, in *Othello*, that information is grossly inconsistent. Therefore, the audience is bound to register that, chronologically, something very strange is happening: time grows and shrinks, grows and shrinks; yet everything somehow coheres. We sense (perhaps only subliminally) that the dramatist is playing tricks on us, yet we acquiesce in them. In the 2006 Oxford edition of the play, Michael Neill alleges that Shakespeare displays 'general indifference to the naturalistic handling of time'; but, in *Othello* (as in *The Tempest*), Shakespeare's numerous temporal allusions actually sharpen our apprehension of the passage of time. When Iago says 'Pleasure and action make the hours seem short', he invokes a 'naturalistic' explanation of a local acceleration. (As for Iago's problematic motives, one of them may be onomastically-dictated racial prejudice: as previously noted, his name is not Italian but Spanish, no doubt honouring Santiago Matamoros – Saint James the Moor-Slayer.)

My point is that our registration of inconsistent information is bound to make us more sympathetic to Othello himself. We intuit an element of kinship. As Othello is fooled by Iago's temporally-impossible and morally-outrageous allegation about Desdemona, we are fooled by Shakespeare's temporally-impossible and egregious presentation of the story. One of the factors which inhibit us from saying, 'Othello, you are a naïve dupe', is our subliminal recognition that we too are being duped, but cannot understand how. Both Iago and Shakespeare exploit the elasticity of the susceptible imagination. Othello's plight becomes more plausible, for it is one which, in part, we share; and his nature thereby seems more akin to ours. As Iago to Othello, so Shakespeare to us: an intelligent persuasive eloquence overcomes the uneasy sense that something cannot be right. Hence we may now infer the following euphonious aphorism: an intimation of logical confusion augments the intimacy of emotional fusion. In simpler English: the vague sense that *we* have been cleverly hoodwinked makes us empathise all the more with the cleverly-hoodwinked Othello. Both of us are tricked by the whirligig of time and a conjuring chronologist.

Note:
1. Thomas Rymer: *A Short View of Tragedy* (London, Baldwin, 1692, but bearing the date '1693'), p. 123.

22

What are the 'Glass Eyes' in *King Lear*?

In King Lear, Act 4, scene 6, lines 170-72 (in my edition), Lear says to the blind Gloucester:

> Get thee glass eyes
> And, like a scurvy politician, seem
> To see the things thou dost not.[1]

Editors who have provided glosses for these lines (G. I. Duthie, John Dover Wilson and Russell Fraser, for example) have explained that the 'glass eyes' are spectacles, eyeglasses. But this explanation presents a puzzle, as there is something very odd about it.

Of course, pairs of spectacles might seem to be grossly anachronistic in the ancient world of *King Lear*. But the world of *King Lear* is not only ancient; it is also modern; and it is in-between, too. Culturally and historically, the play is a temporal muddle. Characters invoke God, Satan, Adam and Eve, and St Mary, so the action seems to belong to the Christian era. The legendary King Lear was, however, a pre-Christian ruler; and characters refer to 'the gods', Jupiter, Juno, Hecate and Apollo: so the action also seems to be located in a post-Roman but pre-Christian Britain. In turn, references to 'Tom o'Bedlam', beadles, and fops who frequently visit the barber, suggest times possibly contemporaneous with Shakespeare's. The Fool even makes a joke of the chronological muddle by uttering a long prophecy and then saying that it hasn't been made yet: 'This prophecy Merlin shall make, for I live before his time.' He surpasses Merlin by prophesying what that magician will prophesy.

A reference to spectacles in *King Lear* is, therefore, not chronologically impossible. Proof lies in Act 1, scene 2, in which Gloucester, seeking to read Edmund's letter, says: 'Come, if it be nothing, I shall not need spectacles.' We know that on another occasion, Shakespeare resourcefully exported them to ancient Troy. 'What a pair of spectacles is here!', cries Pandarus in *Troilus and Cressida*, Act 4, scene 4, beholding the grieving lovers who must part, and punning on the double sense: (i) eyeglasses, (ii) sights to behold.

Obviously Shakespeare had seen in use such aids to vision. Spectacles had been worn in Europe since the Middle Ages. In 1306, Giordano da Rivalto praised them in a sermon. A portrait painted by Tomasso de Modena in 1352 shows Hugh of Provence wearing a pair. In 1480 Domenico Ghirlandaio depicted St Jerome working at a desk from which his eyeglasses hang. During the 15th century, Florence was a leading centre for the manufacture of spectacles.

Nevertheless, the editors of *King Lear* who say that the 'glass eyes' are spectacles have either not looked closely at the text, or have forgotten what spectacles actually do. Perhaps they need to visit an optician.

Look again at that initial quotation from the play, and consider these words: 'seem / To see the things thou dost not'. A person wearing spectacles, on the contrary, is obviously not someone who does not see things, but a person whose defective vision is corrected by the lenses, so that the wearer can see adequately what previously could be seen only inadequately. This yields virtually the *opposite* sense to that invoked by Lear. Spectacles do not fit the meaning of the text.

So what *is* Lear referring to? The answer, I submit, can only be 'glass prosthetic eyes'. Now the sense becomes perfectly apt. Lear is making the point that a corrupt politician *seems* to see certain things (e.g. evidence of corruption in others, or the need for charity) but in reality does not see them at all; or, if he is aware of them, he turns a blind eye to them. The politician thus resembles a blind man who wears prosthetic eyeballs: they make it *appear* that he has vision, although he perceives nothing. A politician with two glass eyes would indeed be totally incapable of seeing (and dealing with) injustice, which is precisely Lear's point.

This is part of Lear's general indictment of corrupt and unjust authority. To imagine that the politician is merely in need of corrective lenses is an insult to Lear's profound sense of misrule. In any case, to clinch our argument, Lear is addressing the totally blind Earl of Gloucester, not someone with merely defective vision. Artificial eyes would have some cosmetic function for the maimed man, whereas spectacles would, alas, be useless. Incidentally, although that word 'politician' could mean 'Machiavellian' in Shakespeare's day, the modern meaning, 'person involved in statecraft' was also implied. George Puttenham in 1589 declared that poets were 'the first politicians, devising all expedient means for th'establishment of the common wealth'.[2]

But could Shakespeare have known about such glass eyes? Did they exist before *King Lear* was written (that is, before the period 1605-7)? In an edition of the *Encyclopaedia Britannica* (1967, Vol. 9), we find that its 'Eye, Human' section contains a sub-section entitled 'Artificial Eyes' which states: 'Glass eyes were first made in Venice in 1579.' The current website of the University of Iowa Medical Museum echoes the claim, though with a degree of chronological caution: 'Eyes of glass were first blown in Venice around 1579.' The *Encyclopaedia Britannica Online* says: 'Glass eyes were first manufactured in Venice in the late 16th century.'

There is, therefore, good external and internal evidence that the 'glass eyes' of *King Lear* are prosthetic eyeballs rather than lenses in frames. And, as has been indicated, this detail is important. The strangely vivid image strengthens the indictment by Lear of the corruptions of power, of the ways in which office may be abused and the mighty may turn a blind eye to human suffering and human need.

The image is a fine example of 'thematic precipitation', which occurs when an extensive theme precipitates a concrete image, rather as a dense solution of chemicals precipitates a crystal which forms on a wire. Throughout the play, there extends a theme of sight and blindness. Lear is blind to the merits of Cordelia until suffering teaches him better. Gloucester has ignored the laws of morality and has suffered horribly as a result. As Edgar says to the illegitimate

Edmund about the Earl, 'the dark and vicious place where thee he got / Cost him his eyes.' In other words, the blinding of Gloucester expresses not only the wickedness of Cornwall and Regan; it displays the workings of a ruthless moral logic.

It happens to be symbolic logic, too, as readers of Sigmund Freud or of David Lodge will know. Gloucester, by illicit (extra-marital) sexual intercourse, has committed a sexual transgression. The punishment is not the loss of his testicles but the loss of their traditional symbolic substitutes, the eyeballs. (One pair of balls deputises for another.) Samson was a sexual transgressor and was consequently blinded. So was Oedipus. So, many centuries later, will be Mr Rochester in *Jane Eyre*. Peter James's thriller *Dead Like You* (2010) features a rapist who is blinded in one eye by a defiant victim. In David Lodge's novel *Small World*, the critic Angelica (who is well versed in Freudian matters) says: 'We are none of us, I suppose, likely to overlook the symbolic equivalence between eyeballs and testicles...', while the novel's innocent hero, Persse, 'listen[s] to this stream of filth flowing from between Angelica's exquisite lips and pearly teeth with growing astonishment and burning cheeks'.[3]

Hence, the invocation of the 'glass eyes' by Lear is further evidence of the brilliance with which, in this tragedy, Shakespeare has sought to give expression in numerous ways, large and small, to the contrapuntal themes of moral blindness, moral vision, and hard-won insight. Gloucester says, 'I stumbled when I saw.' At the heart of the play is the appalling cruelty of the physical blinding of Gloucester; but the work as a whole repeatedly illustrates human imperception and tardy recognition. Lear himself is one who has looked on but not perceived; and, as he gains insight, he denounces all those in authority who, hypocritically, turn a blind eye to the world's injustices. The theme is, alas for the world, always topical.

Thus we learn again that when Shakespeare is writing at his best, every detail counts. Do you see?

Notes:
1. *King Lear*, ed. Cedric Watts (Ware: Wordsworth, 2004), p. 111.
2. See the entries for 'politician' in *The Oxford English Dictionary Online*.
3. David Lodge: *Small World* [1984] (London: Penguin, 1985), p. 323.

23

Who is the 'Poor Fool' in *King Lear*, Act 5?

A notorious puzzle for editors appears near the end of *King Lear*. It is the identification of the referent of the phrase 'poor fool': the Fool or Cordelia? This is no small matter.

The context is familiar. Lear has carried on-stage the dead Cordelia. Albany then seeks to impose a pattern of moral justice on a sequence of events which has repeatedly questioned the belief that moral justice prevails. He says:

> All friends shall taste
> The wages of their virtue, and all foes
> The cup of their deservings. – O see, see![1]

Lear, as if challenging that endeavour to restore moral balance, then cries:

> And my poor fool is hanged! No, no, no life!
> Why should a dog, a horse, a rat have life,
> And thou no breath at all? Thou'lt come no more,
> Never, never, never, never, never!
> – Pray you, undo this button. Thank you, sir.
> Do you see this? Look on her! Look, her lips,
> Look there, look there! [*Lear dies.*

So who is the 'poor fool'? The phrase immediately and naturally reminds us of Lear's Fool, who was so prominent earlier, and who has been strangely absent since Act 3.[2] But the context suggests that Lear should be thinking of Cordelia. We know she was hanged: that fits. Lear proceeds to ask what moral logic can possibly explain her death; and his concern with Cordelia becomes more focused as he looks on her lips and, deludedly, thinks he sees evidence that she may be alive after all. But – 'fool' being often derogatory – why should he address his beloved daughter as a 'poor fool'? The *Norton Shakespeare* editors, like numerous others, say this is 'a term of endearment'. Julia, in *Two Gentlemen of Verona*, refers to herself thus:

> Alas, poor fool! Why do I pity him
> That with his very heart despiseth me?

Here, by 'poor fool', she means something like 'pathetic victim' or 'dear sorry dupe', and she implies affectionate pity for herself as well as for Proteus. In *Much Ado*, Beatrice says of her merry heart:

> I thank it, poor fool; it keeps on the windy side of care.

Here she is grateful that her heart cheers her and repels worries. Again, the phrase implies some affection. The same is true in *Venus and Adonis*, where Adonis, seduced by Venus, is termed the 'poor fool' begging to be released; here there are connotations of 'pitiable victim'. The Nurse in *Romeo and Juliet*, when referring to the infant Juliet twice as 'poor fool', seems to mean 'dear little dupe', 'entertaining child'. The sense 'pathetic dupe' seems to fit the uses in *Twelfth Night* and *Cymbeline*. In the former, Olivia says of Malvolio: 'Alas, poor fool, how have they baffled thee.' In the latter, we find: 'Thus may poor fools believe false teachers.' In *Antony and Cleopatra*, the asp is a kind of dupe in being made to serve Cleopatra's suicide-plan: 'Poor venomous fool', she calls him. In short, the gamut of meanings illustrated in other works contains some support for the claim that Lear may be using a term of endearment for Cordelia which includes the apt sense of 'pitiable victim'.

Nevertheless, objections immediately come to mind. The first is that the term 'fool' has been used numerous times within the play before that late speech in *King Lear*, and in the majority of cases the referent has been the actual Fool, the character. Secondly, and highly relevantly, the very phrase 'poor fool' has been used just once previously in the play (in Act 3, sc. 2); and there Lear was indeed addressing *not* Cordelia but his Fool – so that there my edition capitalises the noun:

> Poor Fool and knave, I have one part in my heart
> That's sorry yet for thee.

('Poor Fool and knave' may be rendered as 'Pitiable clown and lowly lad'.) Inevitably, then, Lear's 'poor fool' in Act 5 evokes echoes and remembrances of the Fool.

But what of the words 'And my poor fool is hanged'? Certainly, that seems to fit Cordelia, for Lear says that he killed the person who was hanging her. But the words could mean 'And, *in addition*, my masculine Fool has been hanged.' Since Lear's thoughts, at this late stage, glance rapidly from one topic to another, a rapid shift to the Fool in the jerky pattern of his reflections is plausible: Michael Hordern showed this in the 1982 BBC television production. Furthermore, the reference then has the effect of completing the story of one of the major characters in the play. (As Sir Joshua Reynolds said long ago: 'It ought to be known what becomes of him.') Apt closure is provided. The Fool, ever loyal to Cordelia when pricking Lear's conscience in the past, now shares her fate.

So, although there most commentators identify Cordelia as the phrase's referent, others identify the Fool. Directors of the play for stage and screen have sometimes evoked the Fool there, too. For instance, at the Chichester production directed by Steven Pimlott in 2005, David Warner's Lear walked ganglingly to an open doorway; and, looking through it, he wailed 'And my poor Fool is hanged', evidently seeing the Fool beyond; then he returned to his lamentations over Cordelia. Again, in the 2001 production by Barry Kyle at Shakespeare's Globe, the Fool's hanging corpse could be seen through the central doors at the end of Act 3, scene 6, thus explaining his subsequent absence and Lear's comment in Act 5.

The eventual 'poor fool' phrase is thus not an ambiguity (if an ambiguity maintains *simultaneously* alternative meanings) so much as a 'duck-rabbit'.[3] A well-known visual conundrum is a sketch which can be seen either as a duck's head or as a rabbit's. The observer can switch from one perception to the other, but cannot retain the two perceptions simultaneously.

Whether Lear's phase evokes the Fool or Cordelia could depend on the director's or actor's interpretation, on our own predilections, or on typography (the First Folio has 'Foole', the Quartos have 'foole').[4] My point is that this puzzle is solved not by eliminating one option but by recognising that both options are valid, so that either may reasonably be selected in practice. Accordingly, I have suggested that the case for the referent 'Fool' is at least as strong as that for the referent 'Cordelia'. Let duck-rabbits breed!

Notes:
1. I quote *King Lear*, ed. Watts (Ware: Wordsworth, 2004).
2.. In Sam Mendes' production at the National Theatre in 2014, Lear (played by Simon Russell Beale) killed the Fool: a drastic solution to the problem of the Fool's absence, with no textual warrant. Indeed, it contravened the text, in which the Fool's last depicted action is to help Kent to carry away the exhausted king.
3. William Empson once claimed that Lear muddles together Cordelia and the Fool; but even if that were the case, we need to identify one or the other: we need to perceive clearly the actuality that he is muddling.
4. Ideally, my text should have combined an upper-case and a lower-case 'f ' ('F' plus 'f ' as one unit) while preserving the visibility of each, but that was not typographically possible. The alternative rendering 'F/fool' (or 'f/Fool') is unsatisfactory, as it imparts a visual stammer to Lear and might seem to prioritise the earlier-occurring letter.

24

'Faith, here's an equivocator': in *Macbeth*, is It Shakespeare?

'Discuss the topic of equivocation in *Macbeth*': it's a predictable exam-question. You can see how it could be answered.

The candidate would initially, if well primed, cite the inebriated Porter, who, imagining that he is keeper of the gates of Hell, says:

> Faith, here's an equivocator, that could swear in both the scales against either scale, who committed treason enough for God's sake, yet could not equivocate to Heaven. O, come in, equivocator.[1]

This shrewd candidate would remark that the lines may refer to Father Garnet, a Jesuit (hanged for his involvement in the Gunpowder Plot of 1605), who had argued that persecuted Catholics were entitled to equivocate during interrogation. Next, the candidate would point out that the three witches, or Weyward Sisters, offer repeated predictions, several of which are crucially equivocal; and these help to lure Macbeth to his destruction. (To those sisters, 'Fair is foul, and foul is fair', phrasing ominously echoed in Macbeth's 'So foul and fair a day I have not seen'.) Too late, Macbeth discovers that Birnam Wood can indeed (as camouflage) come to Dunsinane, and that Macduff was not 'born' but 'untimely ripped' (in a Cæsarian operation) from his mother. The candidate concludes by saying that, to a greater extent than in any other Shakespearian tragedy, the protagonist's downfall is the consequence of equivocation, here meaning 'the misleading use of ambiguous words'.

By now, the examiner's eyes are closing wearily; he's heard it all before. But there's a way to wake him up.

Etymologically, 'equivocation' means 'giving equal voice', as when an ambiguity is well sustained. If *Macbeth* is a tragedy and not a melodrama, Shakespeare must be a great equivocator, 'swear[ing] in both the scales against either scale'. While depicting the

108

wickedness of Macbeth, Shakespeare makes us aware of the admirable qualities in him which have been subverted and destroyed. These are, notably, introspective intensity, martial courage, and a memorable eloquence in recognising his own decline, so that his 'Tomorrow, and tomorrow, and tomorrow' speech can be, for depressed or melancholy readers, what the song 'I Did It My Way' is for drunks in a pub: an enduring consolatory anthem. The grandeur of tragedy depends on grand equivocation; for tragedy stresses the inevitability of suffering and death, while magnifying the value of the beings who suffer and die. The genre is true and false: we are reminded of real woe, but it is theatrically glamorised. Tragedy is consolatory because its deaths often happen eloquently in Act 5, whereas in reality they may happen mutely in Acts 1 or 10. (An 'Act 1' death: an infant succumbing to pneumonia; an 'Act 10' death: a 90-year-old pensioner succumbing to vascular dementia.)

Shakespeare is an equivocator in another sense. While his play commends truth and honesty, Shakespeare cunningly falsifies the moral record of the past in order to win material rewards in the present. To an ingenuous student, *Macbeth* is a tragedy about events in Scottish history which took place centuries before Shakespeare was writing. To a shrewder student, *Macbeth* is a crafty piece of royalist propaganda, whereby Shakespeare's company hoped to ingratiate themselves with the monarch who had recently become King James I. Shakespeare was becoming circumspect, having previously flattered both the Earl of Essex, who had been executed in 1601, and the Earl of Southampton, who had been sentenced to death for supporting Essex's rebellion. Third time, lucky.

James hailed from Scotland, so here's a Scottish play. James preferred short plays, so *Macbeth* is one of Shakespeare's shortest. James touched youngsters suffering from scrofula, endorsing the belief that the royal touch was thaumaturgic; so Shakespeare exalts this superstitious custom by showing that it was established by Edward the Confessor, the virtuous monarch who was proclaimed a saint in 1161. In the play, Macbeth, a foe of James's supposed ancestor, apparently sells his soul to the Devil; but the historical

Macbeth was, according to Holinshed, a ruler who introduced 'many wholesome laws and statutes', so that his people enjoyed 'good peace and tranquillity', for he was accounted 'the sure defence...of innocent people'.[2]

James united two realms; in the play, Macbeth is overthrown by an alliance of English and Scottish forces. The union of the kingdoms is specifically prophesied in Act 4, Scene 1, in the vision of eight kings, some of whom carry 'two-fold balls' (one for each realm) and 'treble sceptres'. James bore one sceptre at his Scottish coronation and two at his English coronation. Indeed, the 'eighth' king cited in that scene is James himself, flattered by a reference to his many successors. James claimed descent from Banquo, supposedly the progenitor of the Stuart line, so Banquo is depicted as brave and conscientious. But the chronicler Hector Boece had largely invented Banquo, Fleance, and the mythological genealogy of the Stuart descent, to support the Stuart claim to the English throne. In *Macbeth*, Shakespeare energetically aids the distortive process, the mythologizing of history in order to strengthen a vulnerable dynasty.

James's *Daemonologie* (1597, reissued in 1603) maintained that witches really wielded hellish powers and should therefore be ruthlessly extirpated. James himself took an active part in the interrogation and sentencing to death of supposed witches. In 1604, Parliament extended the range of punishments for activities associated with witchcraft; and, in the ensuing years, many unfortunate women were tortured and killed. *Macbeth* exuberantly supports James's superstitious beliefs.

It didn't have to. Reginald Scot's *Discoverie of Witchcraft* (1584) had astutely argued that if witches really possessed supernatural powers, they would have used them to gain the beauty, wealth and honour that they so conspicuously lacked. In *The Witch of Edmonton* (*c*. 1621), an old woman is driven to witchcraft by persecution, she being 'poor, deformed, and ignorant'; so some sympathy is won for her. The witches in *Macbeth*, however, are irredeemably loathsome and malevolent. (Even the mellifluous Cleo Laine made them sound nasty in her 'Witches Fair and Foul' number.) King James would surely have been delighted.

The central equivocation of the play is that, while ostensibly depicting the past, it is intensely engaged in the contemporaneous. As an act of flattery of the new king, it evidently succeeded: Shakespeare's company would perform more frequently for James than for Elizabeth. But the flattery itself is dangerously *un*equivocal. While opposing the 'unnatural' and promoting the 'natural', the play endorses the notion that unnatural evil, backed by Satan, is part of reality: *Macbeth* thus endorses grotesque superstition. Shakespeare, so often deemed benevolently wise and tenderly humane in his general outlook, was, in his treatment of witchcraft, contributing to that climate of opinion which resulted in the unjust torture and deaths of hundreds of women. In this respect, Shakespeare did not equivocate enough.

The Vatican's chief exorcist, however, might disagree.

Notes:

1. Textual citations from *Macbeth* are from my edition (Ware: Wordsworth, 2005).
2. I quote from the Holinshed extracts provided in *Narrative and Dramatic Sources of Shakespeare*, Vol. VII, ed. Geoffrey Bullough (London: Routledge & Kegan Paul, 1973), pp. 498 and 497.

25

Is Axing 'a Wife' a Feminist Act?
A Notorious Puzzle in *The Tempest.*

The Tempest contains a notorious puzzle which has baffled editors since at least the 18th century. A relatively recent editor, David Lindley, has remarked: 'This is a crux that can never be decided finally one way or the other.' Nevertheless, my essay presumes to decide it finally. Please recall *1 Henry VI*: 'Let my presumption not provoke thy wrath.'

Some editions of Shakespeare seem to be more feminist than others. In my 2004 'Wordsworth Classics' edition of *The Tempest*, at 4.1.123-4, you find this:

> So rare a wondered father and a wise
> Makes this place Paradise.

Here, the adjective 'wise' repeats the word which appears at that location (albeit with a long 's') in the First Folio text of the play (1623), the earliest extant text. In contrast, in the 1994 reprint of Stephen Orgel's 1987 Oxford edition of *The Tempest*, you find this:

> So rare a wondered father and a wife
> Makes this place paradise.

Stephen Orgel has substituted 'wife' for that 'wise'. Readers may deem his substitution a feminist improvement.

Why the difference? At this point in the play, the speaker is Ferdinand, who, according to Professor Orgel in 1994, is expressing his delight that he has gained not only an exceptional and wonderful father but also a wife, Miranda. Orgel claimed at that time that in the First Folio (F1), the word which at first looked like 'wise' was actually 'wife', though its 'f' had a broken cross-bar and might thus be mistaken for a long 's'. He had accepted as 'conclusive' Jeanne Addison Roberts' argument (in *Studies in Bibliography*, 1978) that several copies of the Folio 'show the letter in the process of breaking'. Admittedly, Orgel's adoption of 'wife' had the disadvantage that a plural subject (Prospero and Miranda) was followed by a third-person singular verb ('Makes'), but this was not a crippling disadvantage. Shakespeare does occasionally link a plural noun to a singular verb, as when, in Act 1 scene 1 of *The Tempest*, the boatswain cries: 'What cares these roarers for the name of king?'.

Again, the reading 'and a wife' may seem to be weakened by the simple fact that Miranda is not yet, with full formality, Ferdinand's spouse. Though Ferdinand and Miranda are betrothed, Christian 'holy wedlock' has not yet taken place. Nevertheless, at 5.1.208-11, good Gonzalo says:

> [In] one voyage
> Did Claribel her husband find at Tunis,
> And Ferdinand, her brother, found a wife
> Where he himself was lost...

This reminds us that although there has been no ecclesiastical ceremony, there has been a plighting of troth before a witness, so that Ferdinand and Miranda are legally, though not sacramentally, bound. At 4.1.1-32, Prospero declares the couple joined by 'contract' ('she is thine own', he assures Ferdinand), but stresses that they must not copulate before the 'sanctimonious ceremonies' – the sanctifying rituals – have taken place. In the judgement of ecclesiastical authorities, although a secular marriage was lawful, any subsequent sexual intercourse would be sinful if it preceded holy wedlock in church.

So far, so feminist, if 'wife' be deemed a more feminist reading than 'wise'. But matters became complicated when a typographer, Peter Blayney, challenged Roberts' typographical claim. In the Introduction to the second edition of *The Norton Facsimile: The First Folio* (1996), Blayney said that the apparent cross-bar on the supposed 'f' in certain copies of the First Folio was only an ink-blot marring the long 's' of 'wise': it was merely 'ink...deposited by metal type on damp paper'. He believed that the physical structure of a piece of type did not permit a letter's cross-bar to break off and drift away, the cross-bar being merely the inked thin edge of a relatively thick part of the metal (think of a chisel-head, and you grasp the idea). The vast majority of the extant copies of the First Folio show an apparently unblemished 'wise'; and, where the word was blemished, this was no evidence of a 'wife'.

Consequently, Stephen Orgel recanted. In *The Authentic Shakespeare*, 2002, Orgel said that although, in 1978, 'wife' was 'a reading whose time had come' (its time being that of burgeoning feminism, as if topicality determined truth!), its time 'may already be past'. In the light of Blayney's researches, Orgel explained that probably a piece of lint had been temporarily caught between the 's' and 'e' of 'wise'.

> Typography, it now appears, will not rescue Shakespeare from patriarchy and male chauvinism. Prospero's wife – and Ferdinand's – remain invisible.

You might think that that would have concluded the matter; but, since we are dealing with a Shakespearian text, the argument continued. David Lindley, editing the play for Cambridge University Press in 2002, preferred 'wife', saying that to misread 'wife' as 'wise' would be an easy error by the compositor or by the scribe, and that what counted was editorial judgement of the more persuasive reading in context. The reader, Lindley suggested, may feel that if Ferdinand were to add 'and a wise' in praise of Prospero, he would be making a redundant amplification. (With a stretch of the imagination, the 'wife' reading could enhance the sense that Prospero, in conferring Miranda on Ferdinand in this scene, has analogies to the God who created Eve to accompany Adam.) Lindley did, however, concede that in a 1999 production of *The Tempest* at Leeds, the director, a *female*, preferred 'wise'. She felt that 'and a wife' reduced Miranda to a mere afterthought. For many present-day readers, that will surely be the effect.

Contrary to Lindley, I believe that the case for 'wise' is fully convincing; and, as I shall show later, it need not demean Miranda at all. Perhaps the most convincing piece of evidence for 'wise' is the presence of a rhyme. To Ferdinand, Prospero is indisputably wise; but what is of greater significance is that 'and a wise' rhymes with 'Paradise'. Indeed, if 'and a wise' seems to be 'a redundant amplification' (as Lindley suggested), that is perhaps because those words were retrospectively generated by 'Paradise': they, serving as a rhyme-phrase, provide its cue. You might object that the soft 's' of 'wise' does not harmonise well with the hard 's' of 'Paradise'. Well, they might have sounded identical in Shakespeare's day; locally, they sometimes do so today: among the sibilant-softening citizens of Bath, for example. (When the disguised Edgar in *King Lear* is speaking, 'swaggered' becomes 'zwaggered', and 'sir' becomes 'zir', as he is imitating a west-country yokel.) In any case, Shakespeare himself provides proof that in *The Tempest* a rhyme is intended. In *Love's Labour's Lost*, 4.3.70-71 (in Hibbard's 1998 Oxford text), Shakespeare uses the identical 'wise' / 'Paradise' pairing:

> If by me broke, what fool is not so wise
> To lose an oath to win a [P]aradise?

If the *Tempest* passage is meant to rhyme, as it clearly is, that automatically rules out the 'wife' reading. In F1, Ferdinand's speech in full, and the opening of Prospero's response, are set out thus:

> *Fer.* Let me liue here euer.
> So rare a wondred Father, and a wise,
> Makes this place Paradise.
> *Pro.* Sweet now, silence: ...

The layout, by not putting Prospero's response on the same line as 'Makes this place Paradise.', renders conspicuous the local rhyme-pattern and thus accentuates the echo of 'wise' in 'Paradise.' (In 'wise' and 'Paradise', as in 'silence', F1 uses the long 's'.)

Of course, the reader may object that Shakespeare would not rhyme a full line with a half line, which would have to be the case here. That objection can easily be over-ruled. This is not the first but the *second* occasion on which, in *The Tempest*, a full line (a pentameter) rhymes with a half-line (a trimeter). The first occasion is at 1.2.441-2. The rhyme-pattern in that earlier instance, however, has been sadly obscured by the editorial custom of replacing F1's 'Millaine' (used consistently and repeatedly in F1) by the modern 'Milan', a custom which unfortunately substitutes a short 'a' sound for a long one. Naturally, readers see no rhyme-pattern in 'Milan'/ 'twain'. In my Wordsworth edition of *The Tempest*, however, I retain 'Millaine', and this renders conspicuous the rhyme at 1.2.441-2. There Ferdinand, explaining to Miranda that his father has been drowned in the shipwreck, adds:

> Yes, faith, and all his lords, the Duke of Millaine
> And his brave son being twain.

Prospero, in an aside, then immediately underlines the 'Millaine' / 'twain' rhyme by repeating the phrase 'The Duke of Millaine'.

Like most modern editors of *The Tempest*, Stephen Orgel emends the First Folio's 'Paradise' as 'paradise'. In the disputed passage, my edition retains the capital letter, partly to respect F1's usage, and largely to respect the theological force conferred by 'Paradise' with a capital. A lower case 'paradise' is a secularised locality. By preserving the theological aura of that noun, an editor can enhance the symbolic aspects of a play in which Prospero often appears God-like; and wisdom is traditionally an attribute of God. That wisdom included the provision of a partner for Adam in the earthly Paradise of Eden.

Stephen Orgel indicated that readers with feminist sympathies may regret the loss of 'wife'. In my view, however, they have no grounds for regret. I believe that Miranda is *already present* in the disputed lines.

She has been wittily incorporated in this Paradise by means of the adjective 'wondered' in the phrase 'wondered father'. Prospero is 'wondered' in at least two senses. First, he is associated with magical wonders. Secondly, and crucially, he is a father blessed with a wonder – with Miranda, the daughter whose name, according to Florio's Italian-English *Dictionarie* in 1611, means 'admirable, to be wondered at', and may reasonably be rendered as 'wondrous'. In *King Lear*, 'childed' means 'being parent of such a child', as here 'wondered' means 'being parent of such a wonder'. Indeed, to clinch the argument: when Ferdinand had first seen Miranda, he had exclaimed 'O you wonder!'. Now, wondrously, the phrase 'and a wise' gains due weight. Since 'wondered' implies thanks to Prospero *for Miranda*, we see that in 'and a wise' Ferdinand is courteously (and tactfully) giving Prospero credit *for his intrinsic powers*.

To sum up. F1's reading, 'wise', is to be preferred to 'wife' for six reasons. 1: There is no typographical case for 'wife' in the First Folio. 2: The adjective 'wise' is more euphonious and is, indeed, essential to a rhyme-pattern. 3: An identical rhyme ('wise' / 'Paradise') had been used previously by Shakespeare. 4: The singular verb 'Makes', gaining a singular subject, fits the syntax more naturally. 5: Miranda has already, within five words of 'wise', been acknowledged in 'wondered' as part of the Paradise. 6: The phrase 'and a wise' is not only a cue for the rhyme-word 'Paradise' but also balances a compliment to Prospero, who is both Miranda's father and a mage. Ferdinand displays courtesy and tact in articulating an elegantly balanced compliment. Shakespeare always relished civilised courtesies: he could be termed 'The Poet Laureate of Politeness' – though he was also, as Caliban demonstrates, the virtuoso of invective.

Thus the editorial choice between 'wise' and 'wife' is no trivial matter. It involves consideration of (among other matters) aesthetics, etiquette, euphony, syntax, thematic implications and sexual politics. Yet, after centuries of controversy, it seems that this is one Shakespearian puzzle which can finally be solved.

26

Prospero's Epilogue: Is it *Really* Shakespeare's Farewell?

At the end of *The Tempest*, we reach the epilogue which (according to the stage direction in the First Folio, 1623) is 'spoken by Prospero'. But does the voice of Prospero give way to that of Shakespeare? Is this really Shakespeare's farewell to the stage? Or is that biographical interpretation merely an old-fashioned sentimental surmise which distorts the literary reality? And hasn't literary theory pronounced 'the death of the author'?

In a modern edition,[1] the speech reads thus:

> Now my charms are all o'erthrown,
> And what strength I have's mine own,
> Which is most faint. Now, 'tis true,
> I must be here confined by you,
> Or sent to Naples. Let me not,
> Since I have my dukedom got,
> And pardoned the deceiver, dwell
> In this bare island, by your spell;
> But release me from my bands,
> With the help of your good hands.   10
> Gentle breath of yours my sails
> Must fill, or else my project fails,
> Which was to please. Now I want
> Spirits to enforce, art to enchant;
> And my ending is despair,
> Unless I be relieved by prayer
> Which pierces so, that it assaults
> Mercy itself, and frees all faults.
> As you from crimes would pardoned be,
> Let your indulgence set me free.   20

In the past, a biographical interpretation of *The Tempest* enjoyed wide currency, and it lingers on. According to that reading, Shakespeare, having made his fortune in the London theatre, was here, in the Epilogue, enlisting the good will of the audience to bless not only his retirement to Stratford-upon-Avon but also, looking further ahead, his eventual departure from the world. In 1838 Thomas Campbell saw *The Tempest* as the poet's farewell to the stage, 'the last work of the mighty workman... Here Shakespeare himself is Prospero'. Then Edward Dowden proposed that 'Prospero's departure from the island is the abandoning by Shakspere [*sic*] of the theatre, the scene of his marvellous works'. Later, Wilson Knight declared:

> Prospero, who controls this comprehensive Shakespearian world, automatically reflects Shakespeare himself...We have seen how many of Shakespeare's tragic themes are covered by him; and that his farewell might have been spoken by Shakespeare is a correspondence demanded by the whole conception.

More recently, Anthony Holden has asserted that 'When writing Prospero's farewell to arms, Shakespeare was consciously writing his own', so that, when Prospero says he will retire 'to my Milan', we should substitute 'to my Stratford'.

Other critics, however, have dismissed as sentimental this biographical approach. E. E. Stoll, for instance, in 1932, declared of the epilogue:

> One hopes that these sorry lines are not by Shakespeare... [The] Epilogue is nothing more than a series of wire-drawn conceits on the subject of pardon and indulgence, and with Shakespeare's own personality and present situation seems to have nothing to do.

Stoll termed the biographical approach 'well-nigh a dogma' and listed numerous commentators (notably Churton Collins and Sir Edmund Chambers) who, in his view, subscribed to it. In contrast, the hard-headed, unsentimental interpretation of the epilogue would treat it simply as an over-elaborate appeal for applause, its gist being: 'If you enjoyed the show, clap your hands, so that we can all go home.' You'll recall such appeals elsewhere. At the end of *A Midsummer Night's Dream*, for example, Robin Goodfellow (alias Puck) says to the patrons: 'Give me your hands, if we be friends': i.e., 'Please applaud now, if you are well-disposed'; and we may recall the kindred conclusion to *As You Like It*, when the player of Rosalind flirtatiously requests a friendly send-off. Why, then, should we read biographically what is basically conventional?

The answer is that the unsentimental reading doesn't work. It does not account for the strange modulations in this epilogue of *The Tempest*.

The speech clearly combines three overlapping layers of meaning. In the first, the character Prospero incorporates the audience into the fictional action, saying that their co-operation is needed if he is to accomplish both his return to the mainland and the successful completion of his project (the project of reconciliation after retribution). Here the *character* draws us into the fiction. In the second layer (which emerges strongly at lines 9-13), the *actor* of the rôle solicits the applause and good will of the audience. In the third layer (which emerges strongly at lines 13-20), another voice is audible. Now, in addition to Prospero begging for help and the actor seeking the spectators' indulgence, it is surely evident that the *playwright*, contemplating retirement, asks the hearers for their intercessionary prayers on his behalf. (The 'prayer' of line 16 may be his for them, and is certainly theirs for him.) The Epilogue's phrasing occasionally recalls that of the Roman Catholic Requiem Mass or *Missa pro defunctis*, part of which may be translated thus: 'Release, O Lord, the souls of all the faithful departed from all the bonds of their sins; and by the assistance of Thy fostering grace may they escape the judgement of revenge'.

The multiple layering, in which Shakespeare's voice is added to that of the character and the actor, is particularly notable at lines 15-18, from 'my ending is despair' to 'frees all faults'. If, first, you think of *Prospero* as the speaker, then the following sense is clear: 'I shall finally be afflicted by the mortal sin of despair unless you successfully pray for divine help and mercy for me.' Prospero has been a magician, and to be a magician was to be involved in a theologically perilous enterprise. According to King James's *Dæmonologie, any* such dealers in 'that black and unlawful science of magic' (dealers who may, like Prospero, 'raise storms and tempests') earned damnation. We should recognise, said the King, that 'their knowledge... is nothing increased except in knowing evil, and the horrors of hell for punishment thereof...'. Furthermore, the title page of the 1619 Quarto of Marlowe's *Doctor Faustus* depicts Faustus, holding a book and staff, standing within an inscribed circle, while a grotesque devil crouches outside it and beckons him.

If, secondly, you think of the *actor* as the speaker of those lines 15-18, then the sense becomes: 'I shall finally be utterly despondent unless I be rescued by this plea of mine, which, if it proves effectively penetrating, will forcefully elicit your mercy and your forgiveness for all the faults of the play.' (In other words, 'Have a heart: please show by your applause that you are a kind and generous crowd'.)

If, thirdly, you think of *Shakespeare* as the speaker there, you find: 'I shall end in despair unless I be redeemed by your acts of prayer, which have the capacity to be so effectively penetrating that they forcefully solicit God, source of all mercy, and thus obtain my liberation from sin and error.' What makes that last reading cogent rather than fanciful is precisely the theological force of the poetry's phrasing. The sense that the solicited 'prayer' is the audience's on behalf of the playwright is supported by the earlier references to 'your good hands' and 'gentle breath of yours'. 'Breath' will be like a breeze filling a ship's sails, but it will also be uttered in good words. Shakespeare often uses 'breath' as a near-synonym or synecdoche for 'verbal utterance'. Various examples come to mind: 'the sweet breath of flattery' in *The Comedy of Errors*; or 'the converse of breath' in *Love's Labour's Lost*; or 'their words / Are natural breath', which we heard previously in Act 5 of *The Tempest*. The capitalisation of 'Mercy', in the phrase 'Mercy itself ', fortuitously or deliberately lends theological weight to the epilogue's plea. In any case, we may well recall Portia's speech on 'the quality of mercy', which declares that 'mercy...is an attribute to God himself'.

There is another way of putting this point. While we are reminded that in the fictional world Prospero must voyage to the mainland, and while the epilogue is predictably and strongly a plea for applause, something else, personal and potently religious, is swelling and deepening it. We sense it if we respond sensitively to the tone. In contrast, the epilogue of *A Midsummer Night's Dream* ends lightly and relatively slightly:

> So, good night unto you all.
> Give me your hands, if we be friends,
> And Robin shall restore amends.

This obviously lacks the religious and personal depth of that epilogue of *The Tempest*.

The autobiographical interpretation of Prospero's speech has ample contextual support. Within *The Tempest*, the analogy between Prospero, who uses his supernatural magic to effect benign transformations, and the author Shakespeare, using literary magic to effect benign transformations, is not only unmistakable: it has also been strongly solicited by the playwright. Repeatedly, Prospero speaks of his magic as his 'art', a term which bridges the activity of the sorcerer and the literary artist. Such art has awakened the dead:

> [G]raves at my command
> Have waked their sleepers, oped, and let 'em forth...

But Prospero has not *literally* opened graves, even if he has caused the supposedly dead Ferdinand, Alonso, Gonzalo and their company (and the mariners) to rise again. Shakespeare, however, has repeatedly caused the historically dead to emerge from the grave of time. Julius Cæsar, Brutus, Cassius, Antony, Cleopatra, Octavius Cæsar, Richard II, Richard III, Henry V and a host of other historic personages walk again on his stage. Their graves have opened; these sleepers have waked. So, logically, those lines invoke Shakespeare, the author as resurrection-man, more strongly than they invoke Prospero.

Prospero leaves the island to return to his homeland; Shakespeare retired from the London stage to die in his home town, Stratford-upon-Avon. Prospero had lived to see his daughter betrothed; Shakespeare had lived to see the marriage of his daughter Judith. After completing his magical endeavours on the island, Prospero will divest himself of his powers. After a highly successful career culminating in *The Tempest*, Shakespeare would write no more plays that were solely his. Certainly, making the biographical analogies less neat, he did collaborate with John Fletcher on *Two Noble Kinsmen* and *Henry VIII* (also known as the untruthful *All Is True*); but then, as Joe E. Brown reminded us at the end of the film *Some Like It Hot*, nobody's perfect.

Shakespeare was a self-conscious, self-aware playwright. Critical comments on actors, acting and stagecraft can be found in *Love's Labour's Lost*, *A Midsummer Night's Dream*, *Hamlet* and *Macbeth*. Reflections on his career can be found in the sonnets: bitter reflections, particularly: 'Alas, 'tis true I have gone here and there, / And made myself a motley to the view'; or 'And almost thence my nature is subdued / To what it works in, like the dyer's hand.' His was a profession to occasion feelings of shame and guilt, particularly in this period when Puritans regularly and bitterly inveighed against playwrights as corrupters and against the theatre as a breeding-place of vice and perversity. London's civic leaders had declared that plays 'contained nothing but profane fables, lascivious matters, cozening devices, and scurrilous behaviours', while Philip Stubbes added that they taught people 'to condemn God and all his laws'. There was good reason, then, why Shakespeare, approaching the end of a long and prosperous career as a playwright, should feel guilt and a consequent desire for indulgence, prayer and mercy.

It is possible that Shakespeare actually played the part of Prospero. After many years as an actor with the Chamberlain's and King's Men, he would have known that the part fitted within his range. Even if, however, the actor were the redoubtable Richard Burbage, who was rather more likely to take such a dominating rôle, the audience could still sense that the playwright's feelings were being expressed through him. (Burbage's name would come second after Shakespeare's at the head of the First Folio's list of the company's actors.) In any case, by now, 1611, Shakespeare knew well that a good number of his plays had found their way into print and were thus reaching readers, not only theatre-goers. He would therefore be aware, when writing that epilogue, of a potential *readership* in addition to an immediate *audience*.

Thus, the biographical interpretation which has been deemed sentimental is actually apt, realistic and comprehensive. It has been given renewed cogency by recent theoretical developments. As I have recalled previously, Roland Barthes's celebrated 'Death of the Author' essay was repeatedly taken literally by naïve academic devotees of literary theory, who then felt obliged to eschew biographical approaches. Now, however, we know that the essay was a satiric *attack* on the outmoded notion that the author should be disregarded. I refer to J. C. Carlier's demonstration in *Roland Barthes*, ed. N. and M. Gane, 2004. We now understand why Barthes, an autobiographer, signed the essay: to reveal its irony and to show his support for the biographical approach. As Carlier has explained, anyone who opposes the ironic interpretation by saying 'But this is not what Barthes intended!' is at once ambushed: thereby, such a person ultimately supports Carlier and the satirical Barthes by invoking the traditional concept of the author and of authorial intentionality. Literary theory has thus reinstated the author.

Moreover, in that epilogue to *The Tempest*, we see Shakespeare providing what, in current critical terminology, is 'metadrama'. Barbara Traister, for instance, argues that the play is 'metadramatic' (i.e. autobiographical), and claims that Shakespeare's use in it of the neoclassical unities demonstrates that 'magician and dramatist both work gracefully within the boundaries of their art'. (See her essay in *William Shakespeare: 'The Tempest'*, ed. Harold Bloom. The neoclassical unities are those of time, place and plot.) Therefore an approach to *The Tempest* which sees it as the culmination of the creative life-phase of a genius is not only supported by common sense and close reading; it is also supported by sophisticated literary theory. Seldom do the three tally so well. As so often, however, we find that the best critical advice comes from Shakespeare himself, in a different play.

Henry IV Part 2 ends with two distinct epilogues, even though editors usually weld them together. One of them was obviously written for a dancer (probably Will Kemp). It begins 'If my tongue' and ends 'good night.' He says that he'll stop when his legs are wearied by his dancing. The other epilogue was evidently intended to be uttered by the playwright himself. That one begins 'First, my fear'; it says that he himself has written the words he is uttering, and that the present play is to make amends for a previous play which was displeasing; and it ends with Shakespeare actually kneeling before the gentlefolk: 'I kneel down before you; but, indeed, to pray for the Queen.'

Here, then, is a precedent for directors. These days, the most effective way of staging the epilogue of *The Tempest* is to let the actor of Prospero, finally representing Shakespeare, again kneel as though in supplication to the audience. He begs them to pray for him.

We thus recreate Shakespeare's astonishingly frank and poignant culmination to his theatrical career.

Note:
1. *The Tempest*, ed. Cedric Watts (Ware: Wordsworth, 2004).

Acknowledgement.

These puzzles were originally published in *Around the Globe*, the journal of Shakespeare's Globe Theatre in London. The editor, Nick Robins, kindly granted permission for the items to be reprinted. For this publication, I have revised all of them and augmented most of them.